Just as he thought his actions were futile, the pup shuddered and took a noisy breath, followed by the tiniest doggy whimper he'd ever heard.

"Was that...?" Ally breathed.

"Yep," he said, holding up the swaddled puppy. Joy arced through him. "It's breathing." He looked at her, his heart surging at the pure relief shining on her face.

"Oh, thank You, God!" she said, then she gripped his arm, her touch firm and warm. "And thank you, too, Drew."

The pup squirmed in his hands, and Drew kept stroking it to encourage adequate blood flow, and to comfort it, as well. Sadie sniffed the pup intently but seemed content to let Drew hold her littlest baby.

He waited with bated breath, and then, after a few minutes, the pup lifted its head and gave a miniscule yowl.

"Listen to that," Ally said, her tone laced with wonder. "What a little fighter."

He held it out to Ally. "Just like you."

Books by Lissa Manley

Love Inspired

*Family to the Rescue
*Mistletoe Matchmaker
*Her Small-Town Sheriff
A Snowglobe Christmas
   "A Family's Christmas Wish"
*Hometown Fireman

*Moonlight Cove

LISSA MANLEY

decided she wanted to be a published author at the ripe old age of twelve. After she read her first romance novel as a teenager, she quickly decided romance was her favorite genre, although she still enjoys digging into a good medical thriller now and then.

When her youngest was still in diapers, Lissa needed a break from strollers and runny noses, so she sat down and started crafting a romance and has been writing ever since. Nine years later, in 2001, she sold her first book, fulfilling her childhood dream. She feels blessed to be able to write what she loves, and intends to be writing until her fingers quit working, or she runs out of heartwarming stories to tell. She's betting the fingers will go first.

Lissa lives in the beautiful city of Portland, Oregon, with her wonderful husband, a grown daughter and college-aged son, and two bossy poodles who rule the house and get away with it. When she's not writing, she enjoys reading, crafting, bargain hunting, cooking and decorating.

Hometown Fireman
Lissa Manley

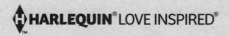

HARLEQUIN® LOVE INSPIRED®

Recycling programs
for this product may
not exist in your area.

™ LOVE INSPIRED BOOKS

ISBN-13: 978-0-373-87815-4

HOMETOWN FIREMAN

www.LoveInspiredBooks.com

Printed in U.S.A.

But if God so clothes the grass of the field,
which today is alive and tomorrow
is thrown into the oven, will He not much more
clothe you, O men of little faith?
—*Matthew* 6:30

This book is dedicated to the brave fireman
in my family's life, Tommy Bonin.
Thanks for all of your help with research—
I couldn't have done it without you.

Chapter One

His eyes on the fingers of black smoke hanging in the rays of the setting sun to the west, volunteer firefighter Drew Sellers pulled up to 25 Flying Fish Lane.

He jerked his truck to a stop behind one of the two fire engines flanking the house. The massive rig ran all pumps on, drawing from a water tender parked at an angle on the road, spraying a thick jet of water on the blaze.

Furrowing his brow—if he remembered right, Old Man Whitley had died about a year ago and the house had been empty ever since—Drew threw open the truck's door and cast his gaze left toward the decrepit cottage-style house set well back on the property. The distinctive smell of burning wood washed over him in an acrid wave.

His heart sank.

The old house was almost completely engulfed in flames already. He wished he could have arrived sooner, but he'd been too far out of town, on his way back from his interview in Atherton, Oregon, to respond and meet up with the rest of the crew at the sta-

tion. But since he was driving by on his way home, there was no way he wasn't stopping to help out.

He ran around the engine, jumped the taut hose and spotted Chief McCoy, dressed in his turnout coat and white helmet, his radio in hand, standing next to his SUV parked on the other side of the engine.

"We've got this under control, Drew," the chief shouted. He waved left. "Can you go see how the home-owner is doing?"

Guess the house wasn't empty after all. With an ac-knowledging gesture, Drew looked to his left and saw a small woman huddled in a dark coat standing just beyond the chief's rig. She held two leashes attached to two large dogs, one black and one golden, her shoul-ders hunched as she watched the house burn.

Sympathy welled; feelings of hopelessness and dev-astating loss were as vivid as they had been on the day his family's house had burned to the ground on the fifth of July the year he turned seven, thanks to an errant Roman candle. To this day, he hated fireworks.

He headed in her direction. "Miss? Are you all right?" He immediately regretted the words; of course nothing was all right.

She shook her head.

He noted the paleness of her face and the downward slash of her mouth, how small and alone and upset she looked. Yeah, he knew what that felt like.

"I'm Drew Sellers," he said by way of an introduc-tion. "Moonlight Cove volunteer firefighter." He looked her and the dogs over. "No one's injured, right?"

"No, we escaped unscathed."

Suddenly, the black dog lunged at Drew, barking, his teeth bared. Drew froze, but thankfully the woman

reacted instantly and pulled back on the taut leash with a quick tug. "Rex, leave it!"

The dog backed off but remained standing, his tail high and quivering, his hackles bunched.

"Sit!" the woman commanded.

The dog whined, then sat, his big haunches plopping down. But his large black eyes remained trained on Drew as if to say, *Move and you die.*

Drew stayed put and made a point of not meeting the dog's gaze. "Looks like you have a protector."

She looked warily at Drew with the biggest set of green eyes he'd ever seen. "Yeah, he's like that."

In between weird heart palpitations, Drew realized he didn't know her, which was unusual since he'd grown up in Moonlight Cove and was at the very least acquainted with just about everybody. She must be new in town, and, well, with those eyes, he'd certainly remember if he'd seen her before. "Remind me to keep my distance."

"He'll remind you himself, I'm sure, but please don't hold it against him," she said, rubbing the big canine behind his floppy ears. "He's had a pretty rough life, and he doesn't like men." She visibly swallowed. "I suspect he was abused by a man."

"So he hasn't been yours for long?" Drew asked out of curiosity, and to distract her from her plight, if only for a little while.

"No, I just started a dog rescue organization, and Rex was my first rescuee." She patted the other dog, which looked to be some kind of chubby retriever, on the head. "Sadie here came home with me yesterday."

This woman obviously had a soft heart and a boat-

load of compassion. "That's a selfless job," he said. "I admire that kind of dedication."

"Well, thanks." She cast woe-tinged eyes toward her burning house. "Although now...well, now I'm not sure what we're going to do."

He followed her gaze with his own. "Maybe it isn't that bad..."

She blinked rapidly. "Again, thanks, but it looks pretty bad to me."

He agreed with her—fire and water and smoke was a horrific combination—but he didn't quite know what to say, so he replied, "Are you new in town?"

"Yeah. I'm Ally York." She flipped the hood off her head, revealing a creamy-smooth complexion, sculpted cheekbones and a cute smattering of freckles across her nose. Long, straight dark blond hair streaked with gold spilled down around her shoulders.

Wow. Pretty.

"I just moved into this place two weeks ago," she said.

No wonder she didn't look familiar. "Old Man Whitley used to live here, but he died last year. Did you know him?"

"No. But my foster sister was his niece, and the house was sitting empty since he passed on, so she offered it to me rent-free. Not sure what I'm going to do now."

Drew's heart lurched—seemed as if she were down on her luck. Before he could respond, though, he saw the chief wave at him from his post. "Excuse me," Drew said.

Drew reached the chief. "What's up?"

"The fire's just about out, but we still have to check for hot spots and bring the debris out."

"I figured as much." He'd had enough firefighting training in his EMT basic class at the Volunteer Academy to know how this worked. The crew would move all the furniture to be sure there weren't any traces of fire underneath anything and then they'd bring the furnishings out of the house to eliminate any risk of the fire starting up again. "You want me to tell her she can't go in?"

"Go ahead," the chief replied.

Drew headed back toward Ally, dreading having to deliver the news. But that was what he did as a volunteer firefighter, what he wanted to continue doing in Atherton, if he was lucky enough to get hired for a full-time, paid position.

As he got closer to Ally, Rex growled low in his chest. Drew stopped dead. "Um…I'm sorry to have to tell you this, but you aren't going to be able to go back in yet."

She lifted her chin. "I understand. Mostly I'm just concerned for the dogs' stuff. They need their food and beds and toys…"

The fact that she didn't seem to care about her own belongings raised her a notch in his eyes. "Do you know anyone else in town?"

"Nope."

Made sense, since she'd only been here two weeks. "Don't worry, I know plenty of people with dogs. In fact, my sister's best friend, Molly Roderick, owns the local pet store, and I'm sure she can rustle up anything you need."

"I'd hate to ask…" Ally said, her shoulders sagging the teensiest bit.

"Well, don't. There are lots of folks around who would be willing to help."

"I'm not used to depending on others," she said. "Guess I'm going to have to get over that." Her eyes glittered as her gaze landed on the attached one-car garage. "Guess my car is gone, too."

He looked at the garage and his heart sank; its walls were charred and the roof had caved in. Empathy welled. She'd truly been left with nothing. "Yeah, it looks like it." An idea rattled around in his brain. "You gonna need a place to stay?" He and his family had been homeless after the fire that destroyed their house, and if not for the kindness of others, they wouldn't have had anywhere to live.

"I'll figure something out," she said, jutting her jaw out. "I'm used to managing on my own."

He dropped his chin. He couldn't turn her loose with no place to go and no way around; that just didn't seem like the gentlemanly thing to do. And no doubt Mom would be on his case if she found out about Ally's situation and then discovered he hadn't helped out. His place only had one bedroom, so that wasn't an option. But Mom and Dad had three unused bedrooms….

"Listen, Ally. My parents have plenty of room at their house."

Her leaf-colored eyes widened. "Oh, no. I couldn't impose."

"Trust me, you wouldn't be imposing. Mom, in particular, would love having you around." Now that Dad had moved into the apartment above the garage, she'd

undoubtedly like having someone else in the house to talk to.

"Would they love having my dogs underfoot?" Ally asked with a lift of her eyebrows. "I can't just desert them. And I should tell you that Sadie here is going to be a mama soon."

"She's pregnant?"

"Yep. The shelter thought she had a few more weeks to go."

He paused.

"If that makes a difference, I totally understand."

"No, it's fine," he replied. "Mom and Dad have always had dogs up until three months ago, when their German shepherd, Duke, died. And my mom has a soft spot for animals. So I'm sure they won't mind. In fact, I think all of Duke's stuff is still in the basement."

Ally studied him. "Why are you being so nice to me? You don't even know me."

He shrugged. "When I was a kid, our house burned down, and I remember how traumatic it was for the whole family."

She cast her eyes to the smoldering house and garage, shaking her head. She froze for a couple of seconds, and some of the light faded from her eyes. Gradually a sense of what looked like inevitability seemed to envelop her like a gray cloud. Clearly, she felt as if her life had crumbled before her eyes, and honestly he couldn't blame her for thinking that. Fire struck a blow no one should have to endure.

Suddenly, Drew had the urge to wrap an arm around her for comfort. But he didn't; he was sure ol' Rex and his teeth would think that kind of gesture was a really bad idea. And the dog would be right. Drew barely

knew this woman, and after he dropped her at Mom and Dad's, he and Ally would only see each other in passing. He had no business offering her any more than a roof over her head, and a part of him wondered why the urge to comfort her had even crossed his mind. He wasn't usually one to establish quick connections.

After a long, silent moment, Ally straightened her shoulders, took a deep breath and finally spoke. "Well, I'll agree on the condition that the arrangement would be only temporary."

He held up his hands. "Fine."

"Good."

He lifted an eyebrow. "What do you plan on doing in the long run?"

She sucked in a large breath. "Maybe I'll…move to a hotel or something."

He liked her determination. But with the talk of her rent-free situation, he got the impression her bravado, while understandable, was false. Not to mention that she wasn't being realistic about finding somewhere else to stay, given that she was bringing two big dogs with her, one expecting puppies any day now.

He nodded. "Unfortunately, there are only two lodging possibilities in Moonlight Cove, and as far as I know, neither one of them allows dogs."

"Oh."

Another idea occurred to him. "Listen, my dad owns a real estate company and has tons of connections around here. I'm sure he could help find an inexpensive rental for you."

"I don't have the money for all the deposits necessary, and until I get work, I can't afford any kind of rent, either."

"No savings?"

"Nope."

Man, she was really in a bind....

"I'll figure something out." She gave him a brittle smile. "I always do."

Again, her determination impressed him. "Okay, I hear you loud and clear." He paused, his gaze on the smoldering house. "Any clue as to what caused the fire?"

She shook her head. "I had the dogs out for a walk. We came back inside, and I was getting to work making more flyers for the housecleaning business I'm setting up."

"This is in addition to the dog rescue?"

"Gotta find a way to pay the bills."

Good point. "Do you have any clients yet?"

"Not yet, but I just posted an online ad yesterday, so hopefully something will come from that."

Sounded like a good plan. "I know just about everyone in town, so I could probably rustle up some prospects."

"That'd be great." She smoothed her wind-tossed hair behind her ear. "Anyway, Rex here started barking, and when I came out to the kitchen to investigate, there were flames shooting from the wall behind the stove."

"Wiring maybe? That house was built a long time ago."

She shrugged. "Maybe."

"I take it you hightailed it out of there fast?"

"I went straight for the door, then called 911 on my cell when I got outside. I didn't even think to grab my keys."

"Good thing Rex was on top of things."

"No kidding." Her lips trembled. "I hadn't even unpacked everything yet." She laughed without humor. "Guess now I won't have to."

Sadie whined, and Ally gave Drew a lopsided smile as she gestured to the dog. "This one is turning out to be quite sympathetic." Crouching down, she put her arms around the dog's furry neck and hugged her close. "Thanks, girl. But don't worry. Everything's going to be just fine. I promise you won't be homeless again."

Drew's throat went tight. Ally was clearly a compassionate soul, and he couldn't help but admire that trait. Once again, her plight had him wanting to come to her rescue, fix everything and present it to her all wrapped in a neat and tidy bow.

Guess he'd need to get ahold of himself and his crazy need to help out Ally and her dogs more than he'd already planned to. Because if things worked out and he was chosen to take the slot he'd interviewed for earlier today at the Atherton Fire Academy, he'd be long gone from Moonlight Cove in just a few weeks.

And once he realized his dream of becoming a full-time firefighter, and eventually a paramedic, he wasn't planning on looking back. For anything or anyone.

Homeless.

The word roiled around in Ally's head like a river of toxic waste as Drew pulled up to his mom's Victorian-style home situated a few blocks from Moonlight Cove Beach. He'd called her as soon as they'd left the scene of the fire, and she'd readily agreed to have Ally and the dogs stay with her. Pregnant Sadie and all.

Ally hated imposing, but what other choice did she have, knowing no one, and having such limited funds

at the moment? Working minimum-wage retail and waitressing jobs in Seattle since high school had barely supported her, and she'd always just scraped by living paycheck to paycheck. Saving money hadn't been an option. Hopefully, that would change as soon as she had her housecleaning business up and running, but without the benefit of no rent, things would get dicey.

Ally's stomach clenched. How could this disaster have happened, just when she'd thought she'd finally found a good place to put down roots after so long without them?

Ever since Sue had described Moonlight Cove to Ally when they'd been in foster care together, Ally had wanted to move here. The town had seemed to embody everything she'd ever wanted in life but never had—a close-knit community and small-town values— all topped off with an idyllic, peaceful life that had been absent from her life for as long as she could remember.

She'd been dreaming of living here forever.

When she'd heard from a friend that the Washington Coast area around Moonlight Cove was in dire need of dog rescue organizations, she'd thought her castle in the sky had become a wonderful reality. Especially when Sue offered Ally her uncle's house rent-free when she'd heard about Ally's aspirations to start a dog rescue here.

For once in Ally's life, things seemed to be going her way. Ha. Now her dream had turned into a nightmare.

She cast her gaze through the back window of Drew's truck, making sure Rex and Sadie were okay in the canopied bed. Both dogs were looking out the closed back window, happily watching the scenery go by in typical dog fashion.

"They okay back there?" Drew asked as he put the truck in Park.

She looked over at him, not for the first time admiring his strong chin, prominent brow and close-cropped, wavy dark brown hair. Very good-looking in an outdoorsy, why-don't-I-cut-you-some-wood kind of way. "Yeah, they both do all right in cars, although Rex usually wants to sit in the front seat of my sedan." Or, rather, the sedan she used to have.

He turned off the ignition. "I'm so sorry about all this."

"Thanks" was all she could say. She hadn't been able to afford renter's insurance, so she only hoped some of her stuff would be salvageable. Not that she had much…but still. For the first time in a very long time, what was hers was hers.

Now it was all gone.

As she climbed out of the car, she fought panic; if her years in foster care had taught her anything, though, it was to try to find the good in almost any situation. To that end she thanked God that she and Rex and Sadie had escaped from the house safely.

Drew came around the truck. "Is it okay to let the dogs out?"

"Go ahead and open up, but let me get their leashes on just in case. They don't know their way around here, and I'd probably have a meltdown if one of them ran off." Even though she had lots of experience dealing with all kinds of setbacks, the fire was a doozy of a stumbling block to the life she'd planned on building here. A girl could only handle so much stress in one day.

Drew opened the liftgate and the two dogs greeted her with wagging tails. As soon as Drew moved closer

to Ally, Rex froze, his teeth bared, and rumbled a low, threatening growl.

"Don't worry, buddy," Drew said, backing up, his hands raised. "I'm not the enemy."

Ally hooked the nylon leash to Rex's collar. "Please be patient with him. He's had a rough go."

"What's his story?"

Rex hopped out of the truck and stood patiently as Ally hooked Sadie's leash on her. "Someone called the police to report that a dog had been tied up on a stake in a yard for weeks on end at a suspected meth house in my neighborhood in Seattle. He'd been without water for a while and was really underweight. They seized him from the owner and took him to the county animal shelter. I sprang him and brought him with me when I moved here." She'd fed him plenty, and he'd put back on most of the weight he'd lost.

Sadie jumped out, her fluffy tail doing its perpetual wag. Honestly, she was one of the sweetest dogs Ally had ever met, so full of trust, so optimistic, despite what she'd been through.

"And what about Sadie?" Drew said.

"She was a stray Animal Control picked up—I think she was probably lost when someone was here for the weekend." From what Sue had told her, Ally knew that Moonlight Cove saw a lot of weekend visitors this time of year. "No one claimed her, so I got her out of the pound and brought her home."

Ally moved away from the truck so Drew could close the liftgate.

"So do you plan on keeping them?" he asked, backing up a step, clearly keeping his distance from Rex.

A cold wind ruffled her hair, causing a shiver to run

around her neck. "Realistically, I can't keep all the dogs I plan on saving."

"You think you'll be able to let them go?" he asked as he walked up the gravel pathway that led to the front door.

"I've thought a lot about that, and I know it will be hard." Agony, actually; dogs had always offered her unconditional love, and there was no question she'd get overly attached. That was just how she was. "But ultimately saving them is more important than how difficult it will be for me to let them go to good homes."

His reply was precluded when the front door opened and a woman dressed in flattering jeans and a bright red boatneck sweater stepped out onto the porch. She was tall and slender, and her unstreaked auburn hair was styled in a smooth chin-length bob that accentuated her fine features.

Undoubtedly, this was Drew's mom, though she looked so youthful Ally wondered if she'd had Drew in her teens.

She waved as she arrived at the top of the wooden stairs. "Ally, you poor thing." Her face was pressed into an expression full of what Ally imagined as motherly concern, though that was just a guess; motherly concern had been in short supply in Ally's life. Nonexistent, actually.

"Mom," Drew said, "as you've figured out, this is Ally York." He turned to Ally. "Ally, this is my mom, Grace Sellers."

Without hesitation, Mrs. Sellers stepped closer, and for just a second, Ally was afraid she was going to hug her. She reflexively stiffened and pulled back a bit.

But as it turned out, Mrs. Sellers simply took Ally's

free hand in hers and squeezed it warmly, resting soft, kind eyes on Ally. "Oh, I'm so glad you and your pups are okay!" She patted Ally's hand. "Welcome."

Thrown a bit off stride by the effusive welcome, Ally said, "Thank you, Mrs. Sellers."

She pulled away. "Oh, pshaw. Please call me Grace, or I'll feel old." She looked down at the dogs, moving forward a bit to pet them. "Well, look at these two darling dogs...."

Drew put out a stiff hand to hold her back. "Watch out, Mom. The black one isn't friendly."

"Actually, he's friendly with women," Ally said.

Grace, obviously used to being around dogs, slowly reached out a hand for Rex to sniff. His eyes bright and soft, Rex sniffed away, and after a few seconds, Grace ran a hand over his smooth black head. "Oh, what a good boy you are."

Rex's long tail started wagging as his butt wiggled in delight, and a moment later he was rubbing against Grace's legs, looking for attention.

Drew snorted. "Well, I'll be." He stood with his hands on his hips, watching the formidable Rex try to get his head under Grace's hand for more petting. "He tried to bite me."

Ally smiled and then turned a sympathetic eye on Drew. "You're the wrong gender."

Drew nodded. "Ah, yes."

Grace turned to Ally with questioning eyes.

"As I told Drew, I'm pretty sure a man abused him before Rex was rescued from a meth house." Trusting a male ever again would be hard for Rex now. Maybe impossible. Ally understood that with everything in

her. She had an ironclad no-dating rule; no way would she ever trust a man with her heart.

"Oh, the poor thing," Grace said before she turned to pet Sadie, who had been patiently waiting for her share of attention. Sadie turned big brown eyes up to Grace and let her scratch behind her floppy ears. "And aren't you just the sweetest dog ever! I'm sure you'll be a great mama."

Ally looked at Drew.

He lifted one broad shoulder. "Told you she likes dogs."

Obviously he'd been straight with her about Grace being a dog person who could deal with Rex and an expectant Sadie. Even so, Ally had to make sure Grace was okay with the imposition. "Mrs....uh, Grace, I have to be sure you're all right with us staying here."

Grace straightened. "Of course I am. I'm not sure if Drew told you, but our house burned down when he was little, and I know too well how devastating it can be." She smiled at the dogs. "Besides, it will be great to have some dogs around again. Lately I've really been missing Duke, our last dog."

A lump formed in Ally's throat and her eyes burned. Kindness always made her weepy. She didn't trust her voice, so all she did was nod shakily.

Grace pressed a hand to Ally's arm. "You've been through a lot today. Why don't you come in and have a snack, and then maybe you'd like to take a rest while I get dinner on the table. The slow cooker's been running all day, so I've got plenty." She turned and headed into the house. "You must be exhausted."

Mentally more than physically. Another home lost was just about more than Ally could deal with. Noth-

ing new there. She should be good at this kind of situation by now. But she wasn't, and never would be. She feared the legacy of her nomadic childhood in foster care would never go away.

Drew stepped aside and gestured toward the door his mom held open, waiting with a gentle smile for Ally to step into the house. Ally froze, the reality of the situation hitting her all over again. She wanted nothing more than to bolt, run away, plant her head firmly in the sand on the beach and never come up for air....

Drew gazed intently at her for a few seconds, his head canted to the side. "Ally?"

"I'm coming," she said, forcing herself to move, even though she would never, ever get used to walking into a stranger's house for who knew how long.

Because in the end, she was just arriving at one more home that wasn't hers and never would be.

Chapter Two

At Mom's request, Drew rounded up the dog supplies in the basement while Ally took the dogs out back to do their business. Luckily, he'd been right and there was some leftover dry dog food down there, along with a few toys, blankets and a huge dog bed. Plenty of stuff to get through the next several days.

Pleading understandable tiredness, Ally said no to the offered snack, and while Mom settled her and the dogs in the guest room, Drew waited in the kitchen as the smell of whatever was in the slow cooker on the counter tantalized him. His stomach rumbled, and he found himself wishing he'd planned on staying for dinner.

Before he left, though, he was sure his mom was going to want to get details of what had happened at Ally's house. He hadn't gone into the particulars when he'd called her from the truck out of consideration for Ally, who'd been sitting right next to him.

Who could blame his mom, really, for her inevitable curiosity? It wasn't every day a fire victim showed up as an impromptu houseguest with two dogs in tow.

Drew gazed out the big picture window over the sink that looked into the large backyard and patio he and Dad had built a few years ago. Given it was April, the sun had set, so Drew stared at nothing but the silhouettes of trees against a star-studded sky for a while, thinking about the air of sadness he'd sensed in Ally. Or was it aloofness? Shyness? Hard to tell.

Just about the time he came back to the kitchen after rustling around in the garage freezer for some cookies his mom had "hidden" there, Mom returned.

"My, that girl's been through a lot," she said, shaking her head. "I think she was asleep before the door closed."

He nibbled on the edge of a frozen chocolate chip cookie. "Yeah, the whole thing is just sad."

Mom went to the cupboard and pulled out plates and set them on the tile counter. "What happened?"

"Ally told me Rex started barking, and she found the kitchen on fire. Ran out and called 911. I got the call on my pager when I was still quite a ways out of town. By the time I was driving by, the fire had already done its damage, so the chief had me check on Ally. She looked pretty stressed out."

"Of course." Mom pulled place mats from a drawer. "I take it she's new in town?" Mom was acquainted with just about everyone in Moonlight Cove, having lived here since she and Dad were married and they moved to town so Dad could start Sellers Real Estate.

"Yep. She moved here a few weeks ago and was living in Old Man Whitley's house out on Flying Fish Lane."

Mom frowned as she got utensils out of the silver-

ware drawer. "Sounds as if she doesn't have a lot of resources."

"Yes, she told me she's on a tight budget."

"I'll have to remember to include her in my prayers."

Funny how that thought hadn't occurred to Drew, even though he'd been raised to pray for those facing difficult times.

Guess he'd lost sight of the power of faith and prayer recently, especially since his good friends Jake and Beth been left homeless in the wake of their house foreclosure, forcing them to sell all their belongings and move to Portland to live with Beth's sister. Drew had sold that house to them and had felt so powerless when the lender had foreclosed. What kind of merciful God took so much away from such good, hardworking Christians?

Mom went over to the oak kitchen table with the place mats. "She sure seems to love those dogs."

"Yeah, she told me she just started a rescue operation."

Mom paused. "Oh, wow. And now she has no place to house the dogs she's rescued. I'm sure she feels doubly responsible for them since they've already been through so much."

"I'm guessing you're right." Ally seemed like the kind of person who took her responsibilities very seriously.

"So, how did your interview go?" Mom asked as she headed back to the counter to get the plates and silverware.

"Great, I think. Since I've already passed the physical, it's just a waiting game to see if I get accepted to the academy." There would be another opening at the

academy next year, but with the tension between him and Dad ratcheting up, now seemed like the time for Drew to make the break from Sellers Real Estate; getting hired and accepted in Atherton as soon as possible had become a priority.

"Looks like you're going to be moving soon, then, just as you've always wanted." She smiled genuinely as she dug a large spoon from the ceramic holder next to the stove. "Good for you, dear."

"I really appreciate your supporting me on this." Drew reflexively clenched his hands. "Dad's still completely against it, but what else is new?"

"Well, your dad is having a difficult time with everything right now." She opened the slow cooker and stirred the contents.

"Is that why he moved into the garage apartment?"

Very deliberately, it seemed, she put the lid back on the slow cooker and set the spoon in a spoon rest nearby. Then she turned, her jaw firm, chin raised slightly. "What's going on between me and your father is not up for discussion."

This was her party line, so her statement didn't surprise Drew.

"It's just that Dad—"

"No, Drew, stop right there." His mom held up a rigid hand. "Whatever problems you have with your dad started long before our current…issues, and I'm sorry for that, really I am. But I simply won't put myself in the middle of what's going on with you two."

Drew tightened his jaw until it hurt, then looked up at the ceiling. So be it; this discussion always ended the same way, and his mom was too stubborn to be

convinced to open up about what was going on with her and Dad.

"I've got to get dinner on the table," she declared, effectively shutting down the discussion. Boy, she was good at that. She started puttering around the kitchen, as if the subject had never been mentioned. Drew fought the urge to push. She'd talk when she wanted to and not a second before. Maybe never, if what had been going on lately was any indication.

Great.

Bothered by their conversation, and his parents' odd behavior in general, he decided to make his escape. He headed over to the far counter to grab his car keys, noting on the way by that Mom had, significantly, set three places at the table. One for herself. No place for Dad, seeing as he and Mom weren't speaking and Dad had been subsisting on whatever he could heat in the microwave in the garage apartment. One place for Ally, of course. And one for...

He snatched up his keys. "Mom, I'm not staying for dinner."

She turned and looked at him. "Why ever not? You haven't eaten yet, right?"

"No, but I've had a long day, and I'd like to get home. I still have some paperwork to do for the meeting with the Sullivans about their offer on the Mayberry house, and I'd rather not be burning the midnight oil tonight."

Dropping her chin, Mom gave him a look that mothers had perfected aeons ago, the one that made him feel about an inch tall.

"What?" he said, even though he knew where this conversation was going. As in not his way.

"Can't you just stay for a bit?" She pointed in the

general direction of the guest room. "That poor girl has suffered a huge loss today, and I think she needs all the support she can get." She *tsked*. "I can't believe you'd even think about leaving right away, given that we've been through the same kind of thing." Then she muttered under her breath, saying something that sounded like...*I raised you better than that.*

He cringed inwardly. Yep, there was the guilt trip she was so good at doling out. Trouble was, it was working, and, as usual, Mom was right. What was an hour of his time in the scheme of things, anyway?

Besides, he was starving, and her slow-cooker concoction sounded a whole lot better than the frozen something-or-other he'd throw in the microwave when he got home to his apartment on the other side of town.

He sighed. "Fine, I'll stay."

"I knew you'd see reason," she said, patting his arm. "We'll let her sleep for a little while and then eat."

"Is Dad coming to dinner?" he asked, just to push the matter.

Mom snorted under her breath. "When was the last time he's been home for dinner?" she asked with a decidedly bitter twist to her lips. "And now...well, now he has to make his own dinner. In the garage." And then she turned on her heel and continued puttering. Loudly.

Drew paused, his brain clicking forward. Come to think of it, Dad hadn't been around home much prior to moving out to the garage apartment. In fact, he been working killer hours for six months or so....

Drew continued to speculate about exactly what was going on with his parents, and if he'd ever figure out how to win an argument with the mule-headed woman standing before him.

Probably not, he concluded, and resigned himself to a dinner with his mom and the pretty dog rescuer resting down the hall.

Though dinner was delicious, Ally had no appetite whatsoever. So she pushed her food around and took a few bites, trying to act as if she was eating; the last thing she wanted to do was hurt Grace's feelings.

Ally wasn't surprised that she couldn't eat; she'd had to call her foster sister, Sue, and tell her that her uncle's house had burned down. Sue had been understandably shocked and upset, and Ally had promised to keep her posted with details about the fire and how it had started as they became available. Sue was going to contact her insurance company about a claim.

Drew was noticeably quiet through the meal, and he focused mostly on eating. Ally definitely sensed some kind of tension between him and his mom, mostly coming from his end of the table. She also noticed that Mr. Sellers was absent. What was the story there? No one offered an explanation, and she didn't ask; it was none of her business.

As soon as everyone was finished, even though she felt exhaustion pulling at her, Ally excused herself to take the dogs out back to throw the ball for them. A tired dog was a happy dog, and she wanted them to be happy and content right now, given the upheaval they'd all suffered today. Some physical stimulation would be good medicine for them.

The sun had set long ago, but the large fenced backyard was well lit. There was a wide expanse of grass just off the patio, perfect for throwing, running and fetching. She set herself up at one end and threw two

tennis balls over and over for Rex and Sadie, finding a minuscule measure of distraction and, therefore, comfort, in the repetitive task.

A strong breeze blew, rustling the large trees at the edges of the yard, and she could smell the scent of the ocean, though she couldn't hear the crash of the waves on the shore a few blocks away.

She lifted her face to the breeze, somehow hoping it could cleanse her of the anxiety and despair nipping at the edges of her mind. After a few moments, Ally let out a cynical laugh; she knew better than to think that she could so easily rid herself of worrying about her uncertain future. Really, though, when had she ever had a *certain* future? Funny how just when she'd thought she'd finally captured that elusive dream, it had been snatched away from her.

All her dreams had gone up in smoke today. Literally. For what seemed like the hundredth time, tears rose and her throat burned. She kept throwing the tennis balls, forcing the tears back. She'd been dealing with crises since her parents had been killed in a car accident when she was eleven; she would not let this fire devastate her. She. Would. Not.

Not surprisingly, poor pregnant Sadie soon collapsed at Ally's feet, panting. Ally bent down and scratched her rounded belly. "Don't worry, girl. I'll figure all this out. You'll have your babies somewhere warm and cozy, I promise."

Footsteps sounded on the patio. Ally turned and saw Drew coming out the back door. Putting on a brave face, she stood straight up, stiffening her neck, along with her upper lip. Better.

"You okay out here?" he asked, his hands shoved in his pockets.

Before she could reply, Rex ran up, snarling, his lip curled and teeth bared.

Acting fast, she stepped in front of the dog and held up a hand. "Rex, no!"

He fell back, his head down, a low, threatening growl still emanating from deep within him. She grabbed his leather collar to hold him still.

To his credit, Drew stood his ground. "Man, he doesn't like me."

She threw the ball to distract Rex, and he went after it. "I'm so sorry. He's just trying to protect me. Maybe we're going to have to work on some positive reinforcement."

Drew cocked his head. "As in I let him get close enough to bite me?"

"Well, yes, but you'll have a yummy treat that he wants more than he wants to bite you, and pretty soon he associates you with said yummy treat instead of perceiving you as a threat."

"I'm going to have to think about that," Drew said, scratching his shadowed cheek. "I'm not sure there are enough yummy treats in the world to change his mind."

Rex came running back, and Ally again put herself between him and Drew. "Sit!" she commanded.

Thankfully, Rex sat, letting the ball drop from his mouth.

An idea occurred to Ally. She bent down and picked up the tennis ball, then held it out to Drew. "Why don't you throw the ball for him, so he associates you with fun. All right?"

Drew took the ball, doubt reflected on his face. "All right, whatever you say."

He threw the ball, hard, and Rex took off after it like a shot. The ball sailed to the farthest corner of the yard and landed in some bushes. Rex disappeared from view and nothing but the sound of him crashing through the underbrush echoed throughout the yard.

"Good throw," she said. Must be that well-muscled upper body of his. Not that she was noticing. "That ought to keep him distracted for a while." And her, too.

"Listen," Drew said, shifting on his feet. He cleared his throat. "I just heard from the chief with…news."

Her stomach dropped like a lead weight. Clear to China. All she could do was nod.

"And…I'm sorry to have to tell you that the house has been declared a total loss."

Numb despair moved in a cold tide through her. She sucked in a shaky breath then swallowed and tried to keep unwanted tears at bay as best she could.

And just like that, there went her hopes for making it through this horrific day without losing it completely.

Drew saw Ally's mouth tremble, and her eyes swam with moisture. He waited for the waterworks to start but, to his amazement, she didn't let one of the swelling tears fall.

He swiped a hand through his hair. "I wish I had better news." The last thing he'd wanted to do was come out here and tell her this.

"Me, too," she said in a scratchy voice.

Rex ran up and dropped the ball at her feet, and she picked it up and threw the toy again. She watched Rex bolt across the yard as she worried her bottom lip with

her teeth. "I'm not sure what I'm going to do now." She blinked fast several times, shaking her head. Still, no tears. She closed her eyes briefly, then straightened her shoulders. "But I'll figure it out. I always do."

Maybe he was reading things wrong, but it seemed as if she were used to handling things on her own. Had she had a choice about being self-reliant in the past?

Admiration for her strength spread through him, along with a healthy dose of curiosity. What had happened to make her so resigned to dealing with things by herself? In another time and place he would have encouraged her to look to God for help, yet lately *he* hadn't even been doing that.

He kept himself from putting an arm around her while he told her everything would be okay. The idea of pulling her close tantalized him, setting his composure on a crooked angle that kept him off balance and slightly uneasy.

Sadie must have sensed Ally's distress; she came over and sat at Ally's feet, looked up and whined. Ally gave Sadie a quivery smile, crouched and buried her face in the fluffy toffee-colored fur on Sadie's head. Ally sniffed and turned away.

Empathy welled up inside him, fast and strong. He shifted from foot to foot and looked at the ground for a second. "Uh, I'm sorry it turned out this way." That certainly sounded lame, considering what had happened, but he'd never been good at offering comfort; it just didn't come easily to him.

"Not your fault," she said into fur, her voice scratchy. "You're just the messenger."

He nodded and kept quiet.

Rex came triumphantly bounding back with the ball

in his mouth, ran in a circle and then dropped the toy about ten feet from where Drew stood by Ally and Sadie. After a moment, Rex sat and barked once, as if to say, *Throw it, you dummy!*

Automatically, Drew responded to the order and moved forward a few steps, his hand out. Rex swiftly stood, flattened his ears and bared his teeth, growling, his hackles raised.

Drew fell back, instinctively snatching his hand in, realizing too late that Rex had been barking at Ally to throw the ball, not Drew. "Okay, boy. Guess we're not friends yet."

Ally rose. "Rex! No—"

"It's okay," Drew said. "He needs some space." And he understood that, better than he wanted to, actually. He'd been trying to get space from his dad all his life, and knew well how irritating it was to have someone trying to close up that space by forcing his wants and needs on the other person.

"He'll come around," Ally said as she picked up the ball and threw it again. Rex took off. "Just give him time."

Time? Drew laughed under his breath. Yeah, right. His dad had proven that time didn't heal all wounds.

"What's so funny?" Ally shot back, her brow deeply furrowed.

"Oh, nothing." He didn't want to unload on her about his problems with Dad, not when she already had so much on her plate.

"No, really." She pointedly glared at him, her eyes turning as hard as emeralds. "What joke did I miss?"

Rex came back with the ball in his mouth, but instead of dropping it, he lay down instead, panting

around the ball, then placed it on the ground between his front paws, obviously played out for now.

Ally went on, her tone rising. "I mean, I just found out my home is a total loss." Her eyes snapped. "Tell me, what could possibly be funny about that?"

Contrition zapped through him. "Nothing, trust me," he said, trying, belatedly, to set her mind at ease. "It's just that…" He trailed off. The last thing he wanted to do was burden her.

"Just that *what?*" she prompted sharply.

He let out a heavy breath. Guess he was going to have to level with her. "What you said made me think that sometimes time can't fix problems."

She stared at him without speaking.

Her silence prompted him to go on. "My dad and I have had a…difference of opinion for a long time, and it's only gotten worse with time, not better."

"About what?" she said, her voice softening just a bit.

"What I want to do with my life," he said, surprised that he was willing to open up. Guess he needed a shoulder, though why he wanted that shoulder to belong to Ally was beyond him. "Moonlight Cove's fire department is volunteer only, except for the chief, so I want to move away to where I can be a full-time, paid firefighter, and eventually train to become a paramedic."

Her eyebrows drifted skyward. "Go on."

"And, well, my dad's had years to adjust to what I want to do with my life, and he's still in a snit about my plans."

She frowned. "Why is he so against it?"

"Well, at first it was just because it meant I wouldn't

be around to take over the family real estate business."
Dad had been adamant that Drew come back to Moonlight Cove after college, and Drew had agreed, figuring he might come to love the business in time. "Then my sister's fiancé was killed while working on a hotshot fire crew a couple of years ago."

"Oh, that had to be rough."

"It was, of course. But ever since then, Dad has refused to accept that this is what I want to do, and he's making no secret of his feelings, either." He rubbed his jaw. "It doesn't help that he moved into the apartment above the garage a couple of weeks ago and he and Mom haven't spoken since."

Ally's eyes went round. "Ah. Okay." She paused, nibbling on her bottom lip. "It sounds like he's just worried about you."

"I know that's part of it. But I'm an adult, with my own life to live. I need him to relax a bit."

"Have you asked for God's help with this?"

He blinked, surprised that she'd brought up the very thing he'd thought about recently. "No." God hadn't helped Jake and Beth, and their lives had exploded. Would He even be there for Drew?

"Well, maybe you should. I always feel better when He's on my team. How's your mom dealing?"

"That's the thing." He shook his head. "She seems to be just fine." He realized how strange that comment sounded. "Not that I don't want her to be fine. It's just that I would expect her to be a bit more upset by their rift, you know? I mean, their marriage seems to be on the rocks...."

"I got what you meant." Ally nibbled her bottom

lip. "Do you think that maybe she's just acting fine to cover up how she really feels?"

Drew thought back to their recent conversations. All had involved Mom cutting him off with a lot of distracting mumbo jumbo and then skillfully changing the subject. "You might have a point," he said. "It does all seem kind of premeditated."

"Well, it's just a thought, but seems like a definite possibility. It's always easier to cover up than open up."

He peered at her. "Sounds like you talk from experience."

Ally paused, her eyes unblinking. Then she pushed her mouth into a tight, fake little smile that didn't reach her eyes, or anywhere else on her face for that matter.

"Um...yeah." She picked up Rex's tennis ball. "C'mon, guys. Enough playing. Time for bed." She regarded Drew, a composed mask slipping into place over her pretty features, as if someone had told her to look indifferent and she was giving it a go. "Good night."

He simply nodded, stunned silent at how quickly she'd shut down their conversation. Her words about covering up versus opening up echoed through his mind, raising his curiosity.

With the dogs following in her wake, she headed into the house, leaving Drew standing there alone with the cool spring breeze ruffling his hair, wondering again what her story was.

And why he cared about what made Ally tick.

Chapter Three

"Hello, Jan." Unexpectedly, Mom's cheery voice rang out from the reception area just outside Drew's office.

His eyebrows raised, he looked up from the Sullivans' offer paperwork displayed on the computer in front of him. What was his mom doing here? She hadn't set foot in the office since Dad had moved out.

Jan, the receptionist at Sellers Real Estate for the past twenty years, replied, "Hi, Grace."

"How is that new granddaughter of yours?" Mom asked.

"Oh, she's just a little doll," Jan replied.

"I'm sure." Mom sighed. "I'd like some grandbabies one of these days. Of course, I love Heidi to death, but I'm really looking forward to having a newborn in my arms."

"You think Phoebe and Carson will have a baby right after they get married?" Drew's sister, Phoebe, was seriously dating Carson Winters, the sheriff of Moonlight Cove. Heidi was Carson's thirteen-year-old daughter, so she was technically a step-granddaughter-to-be. She and Mom had bonded right away and spent

a lot of time together scrapbooking, his mom's favorite pastime.

"They're not even engaged yet," Mom said.

"Well, yeah," Jan replied. "But rumor has it Carson's been ring shopping."

Drew smiled, glad Phoebe was happy and on the path to love after suffering such a devastating loss.

"You might be right," Mom said. "But I haven't heard anything definitive yet." A pause. "Is Drew in?"

"Yup. He's been working on paperwork all morning," Jan replied. "Go on back."

Drew set his mouse aside and swiveled his chair toward the entrance to his office, waiting. This ought to be interesting.

Sure enough, Mom appeared at the open door. "Good morning," she trilled. She was dressed in a stylish pair of jeans and a camel-colored raincoat. Her hair was windblown, which was typical for anyone who went outside in Moonlight Cove.

"Hey, Mom." His eyes snagged on the manila envelope in her hand. "What brings you here?"

"Bank paperwork," she said, holding up the envelope. "Your dad needs to sign."

"He's not here right now," Drew said. "He's showing a house." He eyed the envelope but didn't reach for it or offer to hand it off to Dad. Maybe if they saw each other in person, they'd talk, and maybe that would lead to their working things out. It was a long shot, but Drew would never give up hope that his parents would eventually make up.

Mom held the envelope out. "Would you please give this to him, then?"

Drew stared at her but still didn't take the envelope.

She sighed and dropped her hand. "What's the problem?"

He stood, his hands on his hips. "I'm not going to act as your intermediary with Dad. If you need to give him something, you'll have to give it to him yourself."

Pursing her lips, she stared at him. "Is this really the way you want to play this?"

"Excuse me, but you and Dad are the ones playing things this way. Phoebe and I are just stuck in the middle." Drew ground his molars together. "You two are adults. You need to find a way to deal with your differences without expecting Phoebe and me to tiptoe around, delivering messages." He nodded toward the envelope in her hand. "Or whatever."

Her eyes drifted sideways.

"And don't even think about asking Jan to give that to Dad."

Mom frowned. "Well, aren't you full of vinegar today."

He rubbed his forehead. "I didn't sleep very well last night." For some reason, every time he'd closed his eyes to go to sleep, a vision of Ally standing there, watching her home burn, rose in his mind. He'd tossed and turned all night, haunted by the desolate expression on her face, by the thought of her all alone, with nowhere to go. Essentially homeless. And he couldn't deny that he was still intrigued by her and her story.

Mom sat in the chair across from his desk. "No doubt you were awake all night dreaming up ways to get your dad and me to talk."

"No, actually, I was thinking about Ally's situation."

Mom's eyebrows disappeared into her hairline. "Really?"

He held up his hands. "I feel bad for her. She suffered a terrible blow yesterday, and I'm concerned, that's all."

"Well, I'm glad to hear that," Mom said.

"Why?"

"Because Ally is meeting Chief McCoy at her house in fifteen minutes, and I think you should go with her."

"I'm buried here," he said quickly, gesturing to the piles of paperwork on his desk and then at his computer. "Maybe you could go." Someone should. But preferably not him. Getting any more involved with the lovely and intriguing Miss York would be a mistake.

"Oh, no, I can't," Mom said, standing as she looked at her watch. "I've got a doctor's appointment I can't miss."

He studied her, his matchmaking radar going haywire. "Mom, what are you doing?"

She straightened the collar of her coat and gave him a curious look. "What do you mean?"

"Are you trying to get Ally and me…together?" Mom had made no secret of her desire to see him married with children. He wouldn't put matchmaking beyond her.

"Should I be?" she asked, her voice echoing with a speculative tone that put his teeth on edge.

He sighed. "No, Mom. But you do seem to be trying to get us to spend time together this morning." After an under-the-breath snort, he added, "Before long you'll be talking engagement party."

She blinked. "Where did *that* come from?"

"C'mon. You're a romantic. You've said so yourself." Although lately it seemed as if every shred of that ro-

mantic had gone poof. "You can't tell me you haven't thought about me getting married."

A hopeful light grew in her eyes. "Would that be so bad? Don't you want to fall in love?"

"No way." He'd done the love thing, and it had ended horribly. For him at least. "Love turning out well is nothing but a myth."

Mom pursed her lips and shook her head. "Honestly, Drew, sometimes I don't know where this cynical side of you comes from."

"I can't believe you have to ask that."

"Well, I know Natalie hurt you, but that was back in college."

"Yeah, it was a long time ago." But he had loved her with everything in him. And he'd thought she'd loved him back since she'd been wearing his engagement ring for a month and they'd been close to setting a date.

Until she'd left him for an Italian exchange student and moved to Rome the very day she'd unceremoniously dumped Drew and given his ring back. She'd broken his heart, and it had never healed. At least not fully. His whole being had seemed to freeze that snowy day in January, and it was still numb. Oh, sure, he dated some. But he kept it casual. Getting his heart involved was out of the question.

"So you're not over her?" Mom asked, her brow crinkling.

"I'm not still in love with her," he replied carefully, truthfully. "But what she did changed me inside." He expelled a sharp breath, then segued into another subject by saying, "What about you and Dad?"

Mom froze. "What about us?"

Maybe she didn't know how much their rift had af-

fected Drew. He'd give her the benefit of the doubt and set her straight at the same time. "I thought you and Dad had the perfect relationship, and look how that worked out. You two are living under separate roofs and you're not even speaking." It was the awful truth and had him twisted in so many knots he had to say something. "It just confirms that even the strongest love has problems."

Her eyes flashed, and she opened her mouth to respond. But then she just as quickly clamped it shut. "I'm not discussing that."

Of course not. No wonder she was clueless about his feelings. Everything was off-limits these days.

She belatedly lifted her chin, undoubtedly to strengthen her stance, and then went on. "Ally needs help, that's all." Mom fiddled with the buttons on her coat. "Do I really have to make that clear? Honestly, where's your compassion?"

Chastised, he could only give her a blank look. There was the guilt thing she wielded so well, cutting him down to size with one swipe. Maybe he deserved it. Honestly, right now, he didn't know which way was up with his parents.

Tut-tutting, Mom moved toward his office door, looking over her shoulder. "Try to stop reading so much into everything, all right?" She stopped and turned around, then nailed him with a pointed look. "Just do the Christian thing and help Ally face her burned-down house, knowing she has someone on her side."

His face heating, he watched Mom disappear, feeling as if she'd given him what for. Could anyone lay guilt on like an opinionated mother?

The problem was, his mom's guilt trips were usually

right on target. And this one was no exception. He *was* being uncharacteristically uncharitable. Guess the stress of his life, what with his parents' problems and the upcoming changes looming in his own future, really had him in a funk.

Adjusting his attitude, he closed down his computer with a few keystrokes, grabbed his coat off the back of his chair and headed out his office door. Seemed he was going to be spending the morning being Ally's much-needed support system. Whether he was comfortable with the idea or not.

As she waited for Chief McCoy to arrive for their meeting, Ally stared at the blackened shell of what used to be her home. Rising from the far edge of the house, the brick fireplace was all that was still intact. Worse yet, a huge pile of charred furniture was piled in the middle of the yard, a stark, undeniable testament to the devastating effect of the fire.

Though she was standing twenty yards away from the pile of burned rubble, the scent of fire-scorched debris drifted to her on the persistent breeze.

The smell of broken dreams.

She pressed a hand to her mouth, realizing that she'd somehow hoped that maybe the fire hadn't done as much damage as she'd imagined. But, no. Everything was gone.

She had nowhere to live, with two sweet dogs depending on her. Guess she'd be staying with Drew's parents for the foreseeable future. And while Grace was one of the nicest women Ally had ever met, she was still a stranger. She'd had enough of that to last a

lifetime. But her options were nonexistent, so she'd do what was necessary, as she always had.

Pressure built in her chest. *God, I could really use Your help now. Please help me to deal with this crisis in my life with faith and grace....*

The sound of tires on gravel crunched behind her. With a fortifying breath, she turned and saw Drew's bright red pickup truck moving slowly up the driveway.

Great. Just great. Grace must have sent him. Honestly, he was the last person she wanted to see right now. Oh, he was pleasant enough—very pleasant, in fact. But she always felt so off-kilter when he was around.

Maybe she was being paranoid, but it seemed as if he was always watching, weighing and assessing. And he brought up the tough topics, too. Such as when he told her it seemed as if she spoke from experience about covering up versus opening up. She'd shut the conversation down—no way was she talking about her reasons; that was too painful a subject to share. With anyone. But he'd seemed interested, and that made her uncomfortable.

Not to mention that he was flat-out gorgeous. Those brown eyes and his dark blond hair...

She surreptitiously made an effort to look as if her chest weren't caving in as he pulled the truck to a halt about twenty feet away. After a moment, he climbed out. He was dressed in black dress pants, a white dress shirt and a black-and-blue-striped tie; apparently he'd come from work. What was it about a man in a white shirt and tie, anyway? Just kill her now.

He headed toward her, all confident and strong-looking, and she couldn't help but notice his broad

shoulders under his thin dress shirt, shoulders that seemed as if they could carry any load, anytime.

But not her load. She drew herself up, both literally and figuratively. She knew better than to count on anyone; an endless stream of temporary homes and parents had taught her that lesson early on. Oh, sure, he'd more than likely feel obligated to help her. But she'd seen enough "obligation" in her life to know it didn't mean much in the long run.

The wind gusted, and she shivered as she shoved her hands into the pockets of her jacket. But she held her shoulders straight and tried to look strong. Unbreakable.

He drew near, his eyes scanning the burned-out wreckage that was once the place she wanted to call home. "I'm so sorry," he said, his chocolate-tinged gaze full of genuine empathy that made her throat thick. Surprisingly, he reached out and squeezed her arm above her elbow. "I know how hard this must be."

His touch decimated her backbone. She blinked rapidly several times. Crying *never* helped, and it always made her feel so weak, so vulnerable. She wished he'd skip the empathy; life was less messy that way.

He leaned in close enough so she could smell the faint spice of his aftershave. "You okay?"

No, she wasn't. But she knew the part too well not to carry on as if she were holding things together. "I'll be fine," she said, figuring that if she *acted* fine, she'd *be* fine. Eventually. Maybe. But then again, she'd been holding onto that hope forever, and her grip was slipping.

"You look pale." He put his hands in his pockets as his gaze drifted back to the burned shell of her home. After a significant pause, he rubbed his brow, looked

right at her and said, "Listen. I'm…um, worried about you."

His words swiped an even broader slash at her carefully constructed yet tenuous control. No one had been worried about her for a very long time. "I'm…fine," she managed, barely, not meeting his gaze for fear of losing it. "This is just a bump in the road." More like a giant sinkhole, but whatever.

He said nothing right away.

She looked at the scraggly grass at her feet, wanting with everything in her to run away from his concern. From those eyes. From him. He made her feel exposed. Spineless. As if she needed him. Needing him, needing anyone, wasn't something she could allow. Too much heartache lay down that path.

"Ally, look at me," he finally said.

Swallowing, she turned to him, drawn to his whisper-soft voice.

"Why are you putting on an act?" he asked.

Guess she wasn't as good at pretending to be fine as she thought she was. She'd have to work on that. "I'm not—"

He took her hand and squeezed it, cutting off her words with his strong, warm grip. "Yes, you are. You're pretending to be okay."

"How do you know?"

"Because my mom does the same thing."

Oh, yeah. He was familiar with the move. Just Ally's luck.

When she stayed quiet, he said, "Hey, it's okay to let us—um, *me,* help you."

"Yeah, right." She let out a heavy breath. "I've heard that before," she said before she could reel the words back.

He canted his head to the side, his brow furrowed. "What do you mean?"

She wished she'd kept her big mouth shut. She couldn't talk to him about how she'd trusted others to help her in the past and how those choices had been the biggest mistakes of her life. No way. Those memories were too painful—

Gravel crunched again, cutting off her thoughts, and a black SUV pulled into the driveway. The chief.

"Good timing for you," Drew muttered under his breath.

She pretended not to hear him.

The wind kicked up again, and a light mist started falling. Figured.

He stood there, silent for a moment, then jerked his chin toward his truck. "I'm going to go get my coat. We'll talk later."

She watched him walk to his truck, mentally slapping her head, wishing she'd kept the "Yeah, I've heard that before" comment to herself. The last thing she wanted to do was arouse his curiosity about her past any more than she already had.

She'd come to Moonlight Cove to make a fresh start in her dream town and put her past behind her. She wasn't going to trade sob stories with anyone, certainly not with Drew with his soft eyes and broad shoulders and…everything. Just the thought made her stomach pitch.

As she waited for the chief to come over, she told herself that somehow she was going to have to deflect Drew's interest in picking her apart.

But since she was going to be staying with his par-

ents for a while, keeping his probing questions at bay was going to be tricky.

Even for a seasoned veteran like herself.

Chapter Four

A few days after the fire, Drew stayed at the office late to catch up on some paperwork. The Sullivans' offer had been accepted, and they were on a tight deadline. The sellers had already bought a house in Seattle and were anxious to get things rolling and through closing as fast as possible.

Well, yeah, that was one reason he was behind, he thought as he waited for the offer paperwork to print out. Frankly, his mind hadn't seemed to be in the game since Ally had come into his life. His focus was shot; at the oddest times, he found himself thinking about the heartbreaking expression he'd seen on her face when he'd found her standing there, looking at the mound of charred debris piled in the front yard of what had been her home.

And when they'd walked through the wreckage of the house with the chief? From the desolate look on her face, Drew wouldn't have been surprised if she'd buckled on the spot.

But she hadn't. Not Ally. Instead, she'd put her spine

of steel into action and had simply lifted her chin and carried on.

Even when it had become evident that none of her belongings were salvageable and that she had nothing left.

He admired her grit, her obvious determination to forge onward without betraying her despair. Even as he wondered about its source. There always seemed to be a sadness hovering in the depths of her eyes, just under the surface. Though it was foolish to get caught up in Ally's life, he was curious about her.

Was her time in foster care at the root of her sorrow? What had happened? How had she ended up in the system?

Those questions nagged at him as he gathered the thick sheaf of papers and headed back to his office.

Suddenly, a key rattled in the lock of the front door. He looked up and saw Dad coming in with a wet umbrella in his hand.

For an instant, Drew considered trying to avoid him; it had been a long, busy day, and he wasn't exactly up for a confrontation. That was how most conversations between him and Dad turned out these days. But scurrying to his own office to hide seemed silly, and childish at that. Not to mention that he was tired of walking on thin ice around his father. He'd been doing that for most of his adult life and he was beyond weary with the situation.

Guess that would end as soon as he moved to Atherton. Surprisingly, that thought filled him with disquietingly equal measures of regret and anticipation.

Dad shook off the umbrella and closed it with a snap. Then he looked up and saw Drew standing there. Dad

paused, his brown eyes unblinking, and swiped a hand through the graying hair at his temples. "Didn't expect to see you here."

"I'm finishing up the Sullivans' paperwork for our meeting tomorrow."

Dad set the umbrella on the reception counter. "Ah. Yes." He picked up the messages Jan had left for him. "Heard that deal went through."

For a heartbeat, Drew waited for a pat on the back; he'd done an exemplary job on the Sullivan deal, given how far apart the seller's asking price and the Sullivans' initial offer had been.

However, he was greeted with nothing but silence as his dad read the small pink slips of paper in his hands.

"You know, Dad, the deal almost didn't happen."

"Really?"

Drew ground his molars together until his jaw ached. "Don't play games."

He gave Drew a blank look.

"I heard you talking to Jan about the offer history, so I know you're aware of how the whole thing went down."

Dad's face remained completely impassive.

Drew's neck heated. "Why can't you just give me some credit here?"

"I give you plenty of credit," Dad replied.

Drew stared at him. "Ever since you got wind of my plans to move to Atherton, you haven't been able to even be civil to me, let alone praise me for a job well done around here."

"I gave you credit for years, and look where that got me," Dad snapped.

"This isn't about you," Drew whipped back.

Dad slapped the messages on the counter. "But it is all about you, right?"

"I didn't say that—"

"You didn't have to. Your actions lately tell that story."

"My actions?" Drew snorted. "I'm just following my dream, Dad. Doing what I want. And you always reduce that to mere *actions* rather than anything important."

"And what about my dream to have you take over the business I built from the ground up?" Dad gestured around. "I went from working on the kitchen table to this, and you're just going to walk away from all of it."

Drew felt his pulse in his forehead. "That's just the thing. This place is your dream, not mine."

"Yeah, you've made it abundantly clear this all means nothing to you."

"Here we go with that again," Drew replied. They'd had this conversation up, down, diagonal and sideways, and they never seemed to find any common ground.

"Yeah, here we go," Dad shot back. "I trained you for years, ever since you started working here after school when you were sixteen."

"You can replace me," Drew said with a great amount of control, which belied the rancid churning in his gut.

"Moonlight Cove isn't exactly a hotbed of real estate sales talent. Replacing you is going to be a big problem."

Drew had heard this all before. The story never changed, which only made him want to run away faster. It was a bad dynamic, but he didn't know how to change it. His dad was the most stubborn person

on the planet. Mom ran a close second. "I told you I'd help you with that."

"Now that you've had an interview, it's too late."

"So why didn't you agree to have me look for a replacement earlier?" Drew had offered to start a search several months ago when he'd applied to Atherton Fire and Rescue, but Dad would have none of it. He'd actually forbidden Drew to place an ad or interview anyone.

Dad looked at the floor, then simply shrugged.

Understanding dawned. "You were hoping the interview wouldn't work out and that I'd be forced to stay."

"I'm only thinking of the business," Dad said. "A business that has provided very well for our family, by the way."

But not for the past few years. The tanking economy had put Sellers Real Estate through the wringer lately. "I get that, Dad." It probably didn't help that Drew had chosen to leave Moonlight Cove right now, in the midst of the economic downturn. "But as a prospective firefighter with lots of competition, I'm not getting any younger."

He left out that he could only pretend to be happy hawking designer kitchens and updated bathrooms for so long. No sense in twisting the knife that much. Besides, his dad knew that working as a real estate agent had never been Drew's first choice. Even if he acted as if Drew had decided to become a firefighter on a whim.

"I'm not, either." With sagging shoulders, Dad cast his gaze around. "Who's going to take over my legacy when I want to retire?"

Guilt prodded hard and sharp, and Drew winced inwardly. For just a moment, seeing the slump in his fa-

ther's broad shoulders did a number on Drew's resolve to pursue his dream, no matter what the cost.

Dad spoke again. "Why don't you let me put out some feelers. Maybe you could find a job closer to Moonlight Cove and still work for me part-time."

Impatience tugged at Drew, hard. "Dad, none of the departments around here have any paid positions—"

Drew's cell phone rang, cutting him off. He pulled it out of his pocket, looked at the caller ID. Stacy Sullivan, calling with the last bit of information for their offer. "Dad, just a sec, I have to take this." If anyone understood interrupting a conversation for a client, it was Dad. Business had often come at the expense of family when Drew had been growing up.

He turned and had a brief conversation with Stacy, heading toward his office so he could write down the figure she gave him.

He finished and pressed End, then went out to resume the conversation with his dad, even though he was tempted to run the other way out the back door down the hall. But what was the sense in running from the inevitable? Drew had been doing that for years, and it had to stop.

But when he got out front, Dad was gone and the lights were off.

And nothing but his last words remained, echoing in Drew's mind in exactly the way he was sure Dad had intended—edged in disappointment and so much bitterness Drew wondered if their relationship would ever recover.

Ally moped around the Sellerses' house for a couple of days, occupying herself with taking care of the dogs and not much else. Talk about boring.

No surprise, then, that the walls of her room started to close in on her, and she decided that she was done with the "poor me" routine. Where would that attitude get her, anyway? It was time to move on. And that meant hauling herself up and figuring out where she would go from here. No one was going to fix her problems for her. Only she could do that.

Besides, she was spending way too much time wondering if Drew was going to show up to visit his mom. She needed to be busy.

So one afternoon, she ventured out, lured to the kitchen by the delicious smell of something baking. Rex and Sadie followed at her heels down the hall, their toenails clicking on the hardwood floors.

Ally entered the updated gray-and-white kitchen and found an apron-clad Grace pulling a cookie sheet out of the oven. There was a myriad of mixing bowls on the counter, two open canisters sitting at the ready and a shiny stand mixer sprawled on the island next to lots of other baking ingredients.

Ally's stomach growled; looked as though her appetite had decided to make an appearance for the first time since the fire.

Grace looked up. "Well, hello there." She set the cookie sheet on a pot holder next to the sink. "I'm glad to see you up and about."

Mild guilt shot through Ally. "Sorry I've been so antisocial lately." It had been all she could do to even show up for the meals Grace had so graciously provided.

"No worries," Grace replied with a soft smile. She slid another batch of cookies into the oven. "I know you needed time to regroup."

Ally appreciated Grace's kindness and understanding. Not only had she taken Ally into her home, she'd rounded up some clothes from her and Phoebe's closets for Ally to wear. Grace had also given Ally a basket of sample-size toiletries she and her husband had collected from hotels during their travels over the years. Grace was truly a blessing Ally would never forget.

"I did. But I'm going stir-crazy." Which had to explain why she was spending way too much time thinking about Grace's handsome son. Yeah, that was it.

"I knew you'd come out when you were ready." Grace quirked an eyebrow. "And when you got hungry."

"Yeah, my appetite's back," Ally said as she moved farther into the kitchen.

"I have some leftover stew from last night if you'd like me to heat some up in the microwave."

"You don't have to wait on me," Ally said. Grace had done enough as it was; Ally wasn't going to impose any more than she already had. "Just point me in the right direction and I'll fix it."

Grace did so, and soon Ally was sitting at the breakfast bar eating a bowl of the most delicious stew she'd ever tasted. Rex and Sadie curled up next to the sliding door, longingly looking out at the rain-soaked yard. Maybe a walk on the beach would be in order this afternoon.

Grace looked up from the bowl she was stirring. "Listen, I know you're looking for housecleaning work. My friend Myra Snow had back surgery last week and needs someone to clean her house for the next few months. Would you be interested?"

Ally almost dropped her spoon. "Yes, I would, defi-

nitely." She needed to be busy and she needed money. A job—even one—would be an answer to her prayers.

"Good. I'll give you her number when I'm done here and you can call her and set up a time to meet."

"Sounds great." Honestly, Ally had never encountered such kindness before. She said a silent thank-you to God for bringing the Sellers family into her life.

"And I'm sure if the job with Myra works out, you'll get more work," Grace said as she looked in the oven. "I'll warn you, she's very picky, but if you can please Myra, you can please anyone, and her recommendation will be helpful."

"Thank you so much for all you've done for me. If not for you…well, Rex, Sadie and I would be out on the street." Homeless again. Ally shuddered.

"You're welcome," Grace replied with a kind smile that made Ally's insides go mushy. For once, she liked the sensation.

Feeling as if a bit of her load had been lifted off her shoulders, Ally's appetite reappeared and she dug into her stew as Grace puttered around the kitchen.

Ally noticed the cookies stacked high on the baker's rack by the back door. "Wow. That's a lot of cookies. Are you expecting an army for dessert?"

Grace cracked an egg into the mixer bowl. "No. I'm making goodies for the annual church bake sale." She added something from a little brown bottle to the bowl. "I'm going to freeze most of this, although Drew will complain if I don't keep some of the chocolate chip cookies out for him."

"So he likes sweets?" Ally asked. Although why she was interested in Drew's food preferences was anybody's guess.

"Does a dog like bacon?"

Ally laughed.

"Drew has a real sweet tooth. When he was a kid he used to beg me to make cookies." Grace smiled wistfully. "I'd actually have to hide them in the freezer in the garage to keep them around for more than a few days."

"Did that work?"

"For a long time. But he figured it out when he was in college and often checks the freezer for snacks when he comes over."

Ally stirred her stew. "I can't remember the last time I had a homemade cookie."

Grace's jaw sagged. *"No."*

"Yup."

"Didn't your mom bake?"

Ally's back stiffened. "Um…no." Her mother had been too busy scoring her next drug deal to have time to bake. Not that she'd tell Grace that….

"Oh. That's too bad." Grace pulled a clean spatula from the ceramic holder on the counter. "I take it you don't bake, either?"

No one had ever taught her to bake or cook. That had always seemed like a job for a devoted mom rather than her own neglectful mother or the parade of harried foster moms who had floated in and out of Ally's life.

"Nope." Ally took another bite of the savory stew to preclude having to explain the absence of any kind of positive parental influence in her life. That fact had always been hard for her to admit to anyone.

"You want to learn?" Grace asked with a lift of her well-shaped auburn eyebrows. "I taught Drew to bake, so I'm experienced."

Ally quit chewing for a second, then swallowed, almost choking. No one had ever offered to help her in the kitchen before. "You'd teach me?"

"Well, sure." Grace moved closer and propped a hip against the counter opposite from where Ally sat. "I love to bake and cook, and teaching you would give me an excuse to whip up endless batches of treats that are bad for us."

Ally's throat clogged up. It was silly, but having Grace offer to teach her to cook meant a lot. Too much, probably, but there it was, a testament to everything Ally had missed growing up. For that reason alone, she was going to take Grace up on her offer.

She wiped her mouth. "I'd love that," she said honestly.

"Well, great," Grace replied. "My special double-chocolate brownies are up next, so we'll start with those as soon as you're finished eating."

"Sounds good." Amazingly so. Funny how such a simple thing could lift Ally's spirits.

Grace moved back over to the mixer. "Yes, it does. Especially since if we bake a lot, Drew will be hanging around more." She popped the bowl into its spot and flipped the mixer down and then fiddled with it for a second and turned it on.

Ally hadn't thought of Drew being here more, and she wished she had; she might have given Grace a different answer. But it was too late to back out now without seeming silly.

And without admitting she liked Drew way more than she should.

Chapter Five

Drew stopped at the freezer in Mom and Dad's garage and dug around until he found a bag of frozen snickerdoodles. After he snagged two, he headed into the house.

Mom had called yesterday to ask him to come over and take a look at her computer, which, in her words, was acting "ill with one of those virus thingies." Dad could sell snow to Eskimos, but he didn't have a technologically savvy bone in his body, so Drew had always worn the technical-support hat in the Sellers household.

He hated to admit it, but he was glad he had an excuse to come see how Ally was doing. He'd been wondering about her—who wouldn't be after such a traumatic event?—but he'd felt funny about making a trip over just to check on her. So he'd deliberately kept away. Until now.

The second he came into the family room from the garage, the scent of fresh-baked cookies tantalized the dessert lover in him. Obviously, Mom had been baking up a storm. Maybe she'd let him lick the bowl, or, better yet, have some cookie dough.

He stepped into the kitchen, only to stop in his tracks. Ally was in there with his mom, clad in one of her aprons, a denim number with the words *Kiss the Cook* on the front in bright red letters.

Ally had flour on her cheek and on the front of the apron. Her brow was furrowed, and she looked cute as she worked on cracking an egg into the bowl of the stand mixer he'd given Mom last Christmas.

For just a second, he had the crazy urge to follow the instructions on the apron and lay a big one on Ally. Luckily, he caught himself before he did something stupid.

Mom looked up from where she stood by Ally's side. "Ah. Drew." She gave him a crooked smile. "Good to see you."

"I had some free time between clients."

"Wonderful."

He looked at Ally. "I see she's already got her baker hooks in you."

Ally grinned. "Who could resist with all the yummy smells coming from this kitchen?"

He moved closer, then stopped and glanced around. Sadie lay sleeping by the back door. "Where's Rex?"

"Out back chasing squirrels," Ally said. "You can relax."

He continued on until he could see the brown batter in the mixing bowl. "Mom's famous brownies?"

"Yep," Ally said, pursing her lips. "Although I doubt this batch will be famous except for maybe how many eggshells are in them."

He fought the urge to stare at her lips and bent down to peer into the bowl. "What happened?"

His mom piped in. "Ally has never done any baking

before, so I've been showing her the ropes, including how to crack an egg."

Interesting. Not that everybody was a good cook, or even a mediocre cook. But most adults knew how to crack an egg. Again, he found himself wondering about Ally's background.

"As you can see, I'm not a good student." Ally frowned down at the bowl, then looked at Mom. "You think we should start over?"

"Nah," Mom replied with a wave of her hand. "We've already picked out most of the shells, so they'll be fine." She lifted up the bowl of dry ingredients and handed it to Ally. "Go ahead and put this in and mix 'er up. I'm going to get more flour out of the pantry."

Gingerly, Ally poured the flour into the bowl of wet ingredients, set the bowl down and then reached up to turn the gigantic stand mixer on.

Only, she didn't ease into the speed, and instead flipped the switch right to High. Drew stepped forward to stop her, but it was too late. As the beaters hit the flour, the air around her exploded with flour dust and, seconds later, globs of brown batter, which flew out and splattered her face and the front of her apron.

Ally squawked and flailed her hands at the mixer, but missed the speed switch. Quickly, Drew rounded the counter and made a grab for the switch on Ally's far side, trapping her between him and the counter. But the stand mixer was new and different from the hand mixer he'd grown up using when he baked with his mom, and he fumbled along the side of the machine, looking for the off switch through the dust and brownie goo kicking up from the bowl.

Ally let out a little shriek and pushed back against

him. Being so close to her distracted him for a second and he froze as sparks sizzled. Then, finally his fingers found the lever and he pushed it right, and when nothing happened, shoved it left. The mixer ground to a halt.

After a moment of silence, Ally sagged back against his chest, shaking, her hands pressed to her face.

He grabbed her and turned her around. Was she hurt? "What's wrong?"

Still shaking, she dropped her hands from her batter-speckled face. And she was laughing, her shoulders shaking with every chuckle.

He wrapped his hands around her upper arms as relief spread through him. "I thought the mixer had somehow hurt you," he said.

She laughed harder, until her eyes watered. "I can see the headline now. Rogue Mixer Explodes, Hurting Two with Airborne Brownie Mix."

The picture her words painted hit his funny bone dead-on. He started guffawing right along with her. Somehow his arms went around her, and hers went up to his shoulders as they laughed and laughed and laughed.

Until his eyes met hers and caught, held…

And suddenly he wasn't laughing anymore. Because he was way too close and he was busy falling into her leaf-colored gaze.

Wondering how he was ever going to find his way out.

Or if he even wanted to.

Unable to tear her eyes away, Ally stared at Drew, frozen, her heart running faster than Rex did when

he chased a tennis ball. Thank goodness she wasn't panting.

Drew's hands tightened on her upper arms, sending tingles through her, and pulled ever so slightly—

"Ahem."

Her face heating, Ally jumped back, whipping her head right.

Grace stood in the entryway to the kitchen, smirking. "I hate to break this little party up." After a significant look that made Ally want to squirm, Grace held up a bag. "But I have the flour."

Drew cleared his throat and backed away from Ally. "Great."

Then Grace's gaze fell on the mess the mixer had made on both the counter and Ally and Drew. She blinked. "Oh, dear. Looks like the mixer got away from you two."

Along with Ally's good sense. She cleared her throat and hoped her blush wasn't too noticeable, though given how hot her face was, they might need to call the fire department again. Oh…wait. The friendly local fireman was already here….

"I'm so sorry." Ally pointed to the mess. "I'll clean it up."

"Oh, no worries," Grace said as she got a rag out of a drawer next to the sink. "Nothing that a little spray cleaner won't take care of."

Ally looked at Drew, noting the brown flour dust coating him, and couldn't suppress a giggle. "And a washing machine."

"I'm cleaner than you," Drew said, flicking at her face, his finger coming away with a bit of brownie batter. "Being taller, I was out of spray range."

"But you're wearing a white dress shirt, and I'm not," Ally said, nodding toward the brown-tinged front of his shirt.

He looked down. "Oh." The dismayed look on his face was priceless.

"Yeah. You're a mess," Ally said, pointing at his shirt. "A chocolate mess."

He ran a finger through her hair. "You're a double-chocolate mess," he said, holding up a glob of batter. "And gooey."

Ally touched his forearm and came away with her own clump of goo. "Ha!"

He swatted her hand playfully. "Hey, keep your dusty mitts off my brownie batter," he said in a teasing tone.

The flirty side of Ally made an unusual appearance. "You're not my boss," she returned tartly, darting her hand in to swipe at more batter.

Grace broke in. "Here, you two," she said, handing them clean rags. "If you can stop playing around, clean yourselves up while I work on the kitchen."

Ally suppressed a grin and took a rag.

"Party pooper," Drew said to Grace under his breath as he grabbed a rag.

"Moms are supposed to be party poopers," Grace said. "It's our job to keep everyone in line."

"Oh, she's not a party pooper at all," Ally immediately said. Didn't Drew know how fortunate he was to have a caring, fun-loving mom like Grace?

Drew gave her a bemused look. "I was joking."

Ally paused in trying to get the batter dust off the front of her apron. "Oh." Guess she'd jumped the gun in defending Grace.

"Though I appreciate your coming to my rescue." Grace gave an exaggerated roll of her eyes, then crooked a thumb toward Drew. "This one is always giving me a hard time. I need an ally."

Ally bounced her gaze back and forth between Grace and Drew, fascinated by their good-natured teasing.

Drew gave Grace a big hug. "Oh, come on, Mama, you know you love it."

Ally hung her gaze on them.

Grace hugged him, patting his broad back. "You're right, I do." She pulled away, pointing to the brown dust now speckling her front. "Good thing I'm wearing an apron, huh?"

Drew cocked his head to the side. "Maybe I need to remedy that," he said, then went closer to the mixer with an outstretched finger, as if he were going to dip his finger in the batter.

Grace held up a finger and shook it. "Drew Antonio Sellers, do not even think of flicking that batter on me!"

Ally widened her eyes.

Drew gave an exaggerated evil laugh, his hand suspended over the bowl of batter. "I'll stop if you promise I can lick the bowl when you're done."

Ally tried to envision him actually licking the mixer bowl, wondering how that all worked.

Grace shook her head and backed up, presumably out of flicking distance. "I'm not the cook. Ask Ally."

He turned toward Ally, pressing his face into a speculative expression. "Whaddya say?"

"Whatever you want," she told him, inching back, not quite sure he'd actually fling batter but wanting to minimize the chances just the same. "Just keep your batter to yourself."

He dropped his hand. "You've made an excellent choice," he said, smiling, the corners of his eyes crinkling. "If you continue to cooperate, I might just share the bowl with you."

"I just have one question."

"Shoot."

"How do you actually lick that bowl?" she asked, pointing to the bowl.

His eyebrows scrunched together. "It's just an expression."

She blinked, then dipped her head. "So, um, you don't actually lick it?"

"No…I use a spatula," he said, picking one up.

"Ah," Ally said, finally understanding the concept. "That explains it."

He peered at her for a second. "Do you mean to tell me you've never licked the bowl?"

She shook her head. "Nope." None of her "mothers" had ever had time for baking, much less "licking" the bowl afterwards. They hadn't had time for much at all, most especially not a sullen teenager just wanting to fit in somewhere.

His eyes popped wide briefly. "Well, then you've missed out on a wonderful thing."

A little pang for all that she hadn't had growing up jabbed at her. All she could do was nod. And hope that he didn't ask for details about her childhood. Sharing her story was hard.

"Well, in that case, let's get these brownies mixed and in the oven, and I'll show you how we do things when we bake in the Sellers household."

He set the spatula down, then opened the drawer next to the dishwasher. He pulled out a dark blue apron

with the word *grillmaster* emblazoned across the front in red block letters. As he tied it on, he said, "You game?"

She hesitated. Part of her wanted to say no. But another daring part of her—the part that was beginning to discover what she'd missed growing up in foster care—wanted to experience the things a normal family did. Like licking the bowl. And baking. And spending time together having fun.

Her plucky side won out. "I'm game. Let's bake us some brownies, mister."

"Great." He rolled his sleeves up. "If we work quickly, we can get a batch of chocolate chip done before my next meeting, and we can lick that bowl, too. Nothing better than cookie dough, if you ask me." He gave the mixer a long, appraising look. "I'm sure we can figure out how to use this thing without another mess."

Ally looked around and noted that Grace had quietly, yet conspicuously, disappeared from the kitchen.

Ally's palms began to sweat. She was alone with an appealing man clad in an apron, with batter on his cheek, on a mission to lick a bowl, if only he could figure out how to operate a rogue stand mixer. All for her.

She swallowed, thinking maybe she should have kept her walls up after all.

Chapter Six

Ally stirred the pot of spaghetti on the back burner while also keeping an eye on the meat sauce simmering next to it. Her gaze snagged on the veggies that needed to be cut up for the salad and on the fruit that still had to be washed and prepped. Still lots to do...

Suddenly, the sauce bubbled up just as the oven buzzer beeped, signaling that the pasta was done. Mild panic spread through her. Who would have guessed that making a meal, and having it all be ready at the same time, would be so challenging?

Grace stepped in. "Let's turn this sauce down a bit." She twisted the knob on the stove. "Why don't you drain that pasta in the sink, okay?"

Ally nodded, still feeling very much the novice in the kitchen. "Okay."

"You're doing great cooking your first meal," Grace commented while she stirred the sauce. "It all looks delicious."

Ally dumped the pasta in the holey thingamabob Grace had set in the sink. "I hope it is."

Grace had invited the whole family for Ally's in-

augural dinner, and Phoebe, Carson, Heidi and Drew were due to arrive any minute. Mr. Sellers, as usual, wasn't expected.

Ally flung her gaze around nervously. What to do next? She wanted this dinner to be perfect. She laughed under her breath; it was as if she were cooking for the president rather than the Sellers family.

"I'm going to turn this sauce off. I think it's done," Grace said.

"Great." Ally said, wishing she had three more hands and another brain as she looked at the fruit and veggies again. "I think I'll chop the veggies for the salad."

"I can help with that," a male voice said from behind her. "I'm a great sous-chef."

Ally turned and saw Drew standing there. Her heart bounced, and she pressed a hand to her chest. "Oh, hey, there."

He looked as good as ever in worn jeans and a long-sleeved blue button-up shirt that set off his brown eyes just right. His hair was attractively mussed, as if he'd been outside, and in his hand he held two small bouquets of gorgeous daisies.

"For the chefs," he said, holding the flowers up. "Your favorite, Mom."

Ally blinked, going a bit breathless. She'd never once received flowers....

Grace stepped forward and took her bouquet. "Oh, Drew, they're lovely."

Ally smiled. He'd just brightened her day considerably. With the flowers, of course. "My favorite, too," she said, taking the other bouquet. "Good choice."

"I aim to please," he said, rolling his sleeves up.

And he was right on target.

"I'll get some vases from the curio in the living room for these while you two work on the salad." Grace left the kitchen.

Drew headed to the sink and washed his hands. "So, how have you been?"

It had been three days since they'd baked together, and Ally had seen neither hide nor hair of him since, though she'd thought about him a lot. Too much, probably, given they were just two ships passing in the night, as the saying went. She enjoyed being around him and hadn't forgotten how cute he'd looked with brownie batter all over his shirt. Or the way she'd felt when he'd had his hands on her shoulders, tugging her closer....

With her tummy fluttering, she placed the flowers on the counter and opened a plastic container of strawberries. "Pretty good, considering." Thanks to him and Grace—and God, of course; Ally knew she could count on Him to listen to her prayers, which had been plentiful lately. "I talked to Sue again, and she's working with the insurance company on a settlement."

"Makes sense." He pointed to the salad fixings. "You just want me to cut up the broccoli and mushrooms?"

"Um...yeah. That'd be good."

"Chop or dice?" he asked.

She stared at him, noting his strong, shadowed jawline for no reason at all. "I have no idea." Her cooking cluelessness knew no bounds.

"Small or big?" he asked.

"Small?"

He picked up the knife with a flourish. "Small it is." Without missing a beat, he started expertly cutting up the broccoli.

"You obviously know your way around a kitchen," she said.

"Yes." He gave her a teasing grin, exposing straight, white teeth. "Well, except when there's a tricky stand mixer involved."

"Touché," she replied, returning his smile, her gaze holding his for just a moment too long for comfort.

Feeling flustered, Ally grabbed a small knife to distract herself from Drew by cutting the tops off berries. She was careful to hold it the way Grace had taught her last night when Ally had helped her make dinner.

The utensil felt awkward in her hands, though, and as she tried to adjust the handle of the blade to work right, she wondered at the wisdom of using a sharp knife when Drew was around, making her feel as if she were all thumbs.

Taking a deep breath, she put the knife down and went over to stir the meat sauce. That should be safe enough. "So, heard anything from the fire department in Atherton?"

Drew turned. "Not yet."

She slowly swirled the sauce. "When do you expect to find out?"

"Anytime," he replied as he chopped, having no such trouble operating a knife. "My lease on my apartment only goes through the end of the month, so hopefully I'll know something by then."

"So you're really moving?" she asked.

"That's the plan," he replied, keeping his eyes on his chopping. "Speaking of plans, what's yours?"

Good question. "I've been asking myself that a lot in the last few days."

"What have you decided?"

She returned to the berries and picked up the knife, determined to make another go at cutting them. "Nothing yet." It wasn't as if she had a lot of options at this point.

He stayed quiet for a few seconds. Then he stopped chopping and looked right at her. "I hope you don't mind me bringing this up, but you told me you're working with very limited resources."

Her shoulders stiffened, and she had to put down the knife again. "Yes," she replied hesitantly, still feeling funny sharing so much personal information. Given her traumatic history, she wasn't used to opening up.

He stared at her, waiting, it seemed, for her to go on. She picked up a berry and examined it, then put it back. Maybe it would be okay to share her situation with him just a bit. After all, Drew and his parents had welcomed her into their home, no questions asked. She probably owed them some kind of explanation.

"I've been, uh, on my own for a while." Not to mention that without a college degree it had been almost impossible for her to find a job that paid more than minimum wage. She'd been living paycheck to paycheck for years, holding down minimum-wage jobs. Some months she subsisted on peanut butter sandwiches.

"No family, then?" he asked, his voice low and gentle.

She slid a glance his way as she shook her head. He regarded her with soft eyes and obvious sincerity and concern that made her gut clench. How was she going to talk about this when she was so used to keeping everything in? She'd always been so determined to stand on her own because that's what she'd had to do and she didn't know any other way. "I—"

"We're here!" a girl's voice hollered from the front of the house.

Ally clamped her mouth shut, feeling an odd mix of relief and disappointment that shoved her even more off balance.

"We'll talk later," he said quietly just as a blonde girl who looked to be around twelve or thirteen ran into the kitchen.

"I heard there are dogs staying here!" she said, her voice dripping with excitement. She glanced around. "Where are they?"

"Well, hello to you, too, Heidi, Heidi Bo-bidy," Drew said in a teasing tone. "Since when are dogs more important than me?"

The girl laughed. "Hey, Drew, Drew Bo-boo," she said, skipping over. Without hesitation, she threw her arms around him and gave him a big hug.

Drew hugged her back, lifting her off her feet. "Whoa," he said. "You've grown since the last time I saw you, Bo-bidy. Must be all that ice cream you eat at Phoebe's store."

Heidi giggled as he set her on her feet. "Yup. I get paid in all the ice cream I want."

Ally couldn't take her eyes off them, the big firefighter hugging this little blonde dynamo. She cleared her throat, focusing on the most obvious question at hand. "Bo-bidy?" she said, angling one brow up.

Heidi looked at her, smiling, her blue eyes sparkling. "It's from a song Drew taught me."

Ally frowned.

"You know. 'The Name Game' song?" He proceeded to spew out a mouthful of words that rhymed with *Heidi* in a singsong voice.

Heidi did the same, using Drew's name. Both of them laughed uproariously when she was done, and then they high-fived each other.

"Good job!" Drew said. "You've got it down. Now let me introduce you to the very nice lady who owns those two dogs you're so interested in seeing."

He made the introductions, and then he and Heidi went off to drag the rest of the family into the kitchen.

As they walked away—the tall, dark, broad-shouldered man and the short blonde girl bouncing along beside him—Ally stared at them. She simply couldn't get over how they'd interacted. Hugging. Teasing. Cute inside jokes and songs.

She shook her head. Drew was wonderful with Heidi. Really wonderful. He was definitely worth a second look.

For anyone but Ally.

Drew looked out the window over the sink, trying not to make it too obvious that he was watching Ally and Heidi play with Rex and Sadie. Well, mostly he was watching Ally.

He could hear their shrieks of delight echoing through the early evening air, especially Heidi's as she ran around and Rex jubilantly chased her, nipping at her heels and yipping in delight. Ally stood back with Sadie, laughing at Rex's antics, her face lit up with a brilliant smile.

"They're really having fun," Phoebe said behind him.

He turned. "Yeah. Thanks for taking over for Ally in the kitchen so she could go out and introduce Heidi to the dogs." Carson was down in the basement with

Mom, helping her change the furnace filter. Dad wasn't around enough to do many household chores, and hadn't been for a while.

"Hey, no problem. Ally looked a little overwhelmed by all this," she said, gesturing around the kitchen.

"Yeah, she's just learning to cook."

"That's what Mom said." Phoebe picked up a berry. "She seems nice."

"Yup," Drew said before he went to the fridge to get the salad dressing out.

"Pretty, too." Phoebe's voice oozed casualness that made her question far from actually being casual.

Oh, boy. Here came the interrogation. "That, too."

"Single, right?"

"Yep." He put the salad and the dressing on the counter to be taken in to the dining room.

"Obviously compassionate, if she rescues homeless dogs."

"Guess so."

"She looks to be about your age."

"Not sure."

Phoebe looked out the window at Heidi and Ally. "She seems to like kids."

"Looks that way."

Dead silence.

Drew finally rolled his eyes as he grabbed the salad. "Why don't you go ahead and say it."

Phoebe made a face rife with innocence. "Say what?"

"Oh, come on, Phoebs. You think I should be interested in her."

"I didn't say that," she said, examining a strawberry as if it was speckled in gold.

"You didn't have to. Your little cross-examination spoke for itself."

"I was not cross-examining you." She flipped the berry into the bowl. "Well, maybe I kinda was."

"Kinda?" He snorted. "You covered her personality, marital status, attractiveness, age and her skills with kids." He pierced Phoebe with a dagger-sharp stare. "If that isn't an interrogation, I'm a hippopotamus dressed in high heels and a skirt."

Phoebe shrugged. "Okay, so I'm interested in her." A pause. "Are you?"

He grabbed a berry and popped it in his mouth. "I take it you think I should be." Ever since Phoebe had fallen in love with Carson, she saw hearts and flowers everywhere. Drew had stopped being that idealistic years ago. Failed love had a way of doing that.

"Well, yeah," she replied, as if he'd asked her if the sky was blue. "You need some romance in your life."

"Okay, I'll bite. Why do you think I need romance?" For some odd reason, he was interested in her perspective.

She turned dreamy eyes on him. "Because it's *wonderful*."

He smiled. "I'm glad you're so happy, sis, really I am. But love isn't always wonderful. You of all people should understand that." After her fiancé died, Phoebe had firmly believed there were no second chances in love.

"You fought falling for Carson tooth and nail, and you sure didn't like it when Molly did her matchmaking thing to you." Molly Roderick, Phoebe's best friend and the most successful matchmaker in Moonlight Cove,

had initially been the one to push Phoebe toward dating Carson, the handsome new sheriff in town at the time.

"I know, I remember," Phoebe replied. "But I can look back on that now and see that all of my fighting Molly, and myself, was a waste of time. Second chances do exist—Carson and I are proof of that." She speared Drew with her baby-blue gaze. "Take it from me. The right person is out there for you."

"And you think it might be Ally?" he asked, almost afraid to hear Phoebe's answer, a bit surprised he'd even posed the question. Ally, it seemed, had worked her way under his skin more than he'd thought. Not good.

"Maybe, maybe not." Phoebe turned on the faucet to wash her knife. "But how will you know unless you give her a chance?"

She made a good point. Which prompted him to change the subject slightly by saying, "Have you forgotten I'm leaving town soon?"

"So that Atherton Fire Department thing is a go?"

"Getting close," he replied. "My interview last week went really well."

"That's great," she said, patting his shoulder. "How's Dad dealing with that?"

"Not well, but no surprise there."

"So he hasn't come around at all?" She took the fruit salad to the counter.

"Nope." Drew doubted he ever would. "But I'm doing what I need to whether he's with me or not. I can't live my life waiting for his approval."

Phoebe propped a hip against the counter. "Good for you."

"Thanks."

She pinned him in place with a knowing stare. "So,

now that you've changed the subject, let's get back to you and Ally."

Busted. "Never could hide anything from you, could I?"

"Not a chance," she said with a grin. "As I was saying, don't waste time making up reasons not to be interested in Ally."

He just looked at her, one brow at an angle.

"You can give me all the excuses in the world, but I know what you're doing because I was the same way. If you spend all your time rationalizing why you and Ally—or anyone, for that matter—would never work, you might be missing out on something wonderful."

Before he could toss Phoebe a profound rejoinder, the back door opened, and Heidi barreled through and tore into the kitchen, then back out again, Rex at her heels, his toenails clickety-clacking on the tile floor. As soon as he spotted Phoebe, he changed course and ran over, his tail wagging. Until he saw Drew. Instantaneously, Rex skidded to a stop on the hardwood, his head going down, a deep growl emanating from his chest.

Phoebe whistled under her breath. "Wow. He doesn't like you, does he?" She reached down and soothed the dog.

"Nope."

"You think he ever will?"

Drew went for the smelly dog treats on the counter Ally had told him to give Rex. "Ally and I are working on positive reinforcement."

"Maybe you should do the same."

Drew swung his head toward his sister, the treats forgotten. "Huh?"

"Spend some time with Ally," Phoebe counseled solemnly, her voice going soft. "Maybe you'll discover, as I did, that letting someone into your heart has more positives than negatives."

He looked at the ceiling and let out a heavy sigh. Trouble was, that's exactly what he was afraid of. And with a new job on the line and his dream finally within reach, he wasn't sure making that discovery would be a good thing for him at all.

Chapter Seven

"So, when is Sadie going to have her babies?" Heidi asked Ally in between bites of spaghetti. "She looks chubby."

Everyone had finally gathered around the table in the dining room to eat the meal Ally had mostly prepared. No one had run from the table, gagging, or fallen over dead, so she assumed the food was acceptable.

"I'm not sure, exactly, but soon," Ally replied, giving Heidi a gentle smile. "She was pregnant when I rescued her, so there's been a little bit of guesswork on when the puppies will actually arrive."

A pause. "What are you going to do with them after they're born?" Heidi asked with a sideways look that spelled *interest* in big black letters.

"Find them good homes when they're old enough," Ally replied. "She looks like a purebred golden retriever, so hopefully it won't be too difficult to place them."

Heidi turned big blue eyes to Carson. "Dad, could we have one?"

Carson paused, his spaghetti-laden fork halfway to

his mouth. "Um…I don't know." He looked to Phoebe. "What do you think?"

Phoebe looked up from buttering her bread. "You're asking me?"

"Well, yeah," Carson said. "I'd really like your opinion."

"Oh, well, I love dogs, obviously." Phoebe set her fork down. "But…this should be your decision."

"But what do you think?" Carson asked, leaning a forearm on the edge of the table.

"I'll go with whatever you want," Phoebe replied.

Heidi piped in. "Come on, Phoebe. I want you on my side." She put her hands together in front of her. "Please, please, please?"

"Let Phoebe decide for herself," Carson interjected.

Phoebe looked back and forth between father and daughter. "Wow, this is a lot of pressure."

"Guess you better get used to pressure," Carson said.

Phoebe looked confused. "Why?"

Carson paused. "That's what parents face every day."

"Parents?" Phoebe nervously shoved some of her curly hair behind one ear. "Um…what do you mean by that?"

A hush fell over the room.

Carson cleared his throat. "Well, I was going to save this for later. But now seems like a good time to make it official."

"Make what official?" Phoebe said in a strangled voice.

"This," Carson said as he pulled a velvet-covered black box out of his pocket.

Her heart stalled, Ally watched in rapt awe as he

got down on one knee next to Phoebe and took her hand in his.

Phoebe's jaw dropped low as she pressed a hand to her chest. Heidi bounced up and down in her chair, her face glowing.

"Phoebe Sellers, I love you." Carson flipped the box open with his thumb, exposing a gorgeous round diamond solitaire set in white gold. "And I want to spend the rest of my life with you." He reached up and stroked her cheek. "Will you make me the happiest man on earth and marry me?"

A gasp came from Grace at the end of the table, and then Ally saw tears form in Phoebe's eyes. But Ally knew without a doubt that they were nothing less than tears of sheer joy.

Phoebe nodded her head, pushing her long, curly blond hair back with one visibly trembling hand. "Yes, yes, you amazing man. Of course I'll marry you!"

Heidi looked as if she was going to be the one having puppies; her face glowed and her eyes shone with pure, giddy happiness. Obviously she was thrilled with this turn of events.

Ally's heart fluttered; she could only imagine how wonderful it must be for Heidi to have someone like Phoebe as her mom, someone who would love her unconditionally and completely and would never leave her. Ally would be shouting the news from the rooftops. To Heidi's credit, she stayed quiet—barely—while the romantic scene played out.

Carson took the ring out of the box with a noticeably shaky grip and gently pushed it onto Phoebe's left ring finger.

"It fits perfectly," Phoebe said as she admired the ring on her finger, her face aglow.

"A perfect ring for the perfect woman," Carson said, stroking her cheek, his brown eyes radiating pure adoration. "I can't wait for you to be my wife."

Phoebe gazed up at Carson, her eyes glittering. "How did I ever find you?"

"God brought us together," he said simply.

She nodded as tears crested and ran down her flushed cheeks. And then without a word she threw herself into his arms, sobbing, burying her face in his neck. His arms came around her and held her close, and he bent his head and whispered something in her ear.

Ally got to her feet and watched the happy clutch from the end of the table, her eyes burning.

Heidi cheered, Grace rose and walked over to hug Phoebe, and Drew beamed with happiness. Pretty soon the whole group was hugging and shaking hands and congratulating and crying, or in Grace's case, blubbering.

Drew pointed at Heidi. "Hey, Bo-bidy. Looks like I'm gonna be your uncle! How cool is that?"

"So cool!" Heidi said, giving him a thumbs-up. "And how cool is it that I'm going to have a mom again?"

As Ally stood there by herself watching the happy scene play out just as it should, her chest clenched.

Have a mom again.

The words seared her, for she'd never been able to say them.

She was happy for everyone here, of course. But, as usual, she was on the outside looking in, a peripheral witness to others' happiness, but not an actual part of

it. She bit her lip as she smiled, determined not to ruin this moment for everyone else with her own self-pity.

Sadie wandered over and gave Ally a long, significant look.

"You need to go out, girl?"

Sadie answered by waddling toward the back door, looking back at Ally once, her big dark eyes pleading as her tail wagged ever so slightly. Pregnant mama dog needed a potty break.

Good excuse to take a time-out. Ally needed a breather, too. Quietly she headed toward the door, pausing while she wondered if she would ever find the kind of happiness Carson, Phoebe and Heidi had.

She laughed under her breath. Somehow she was afraid all the time-outs in the world would never be enough to make that kind of pie-in-the-sky dream come true.

Drew looked up from hugging Phoebe and saw Ally leave the dining room, her shoulders riding a bit low. He let Phoebe go, craned his head and observed Ally following Sadie to the back door. Oh, okay. Sadie needed to go out.

Ally stopped at the door, paused and then threw a lingering look back into the dining room, her expression ever-so-slightly tinged with…sadness? Resignation?

Longing?

Before he could figure the puzzle out, her gaze collided with his—*bam!*—and she froze for a split second, her eyes wide and unblinking. As if he'd caught her with her hand in the cookie jar.

Or witnessed a reaction she hadn't planned on him seeing…?

He twitched his eyebrows together as he held her gaze, and then her face cleared, her shoulders straightened and she flicked up the corners of her mouth in a bright yet stiff smile. She turned and went out the door.

He frowned as happy conversation swirled around him. Had her smile seemed fake? Forced? Yeah. Definitely. His curiosity radar pinged, and before he could stop himself, he was walking after her, reassuring himself with a quick glance Heidi's way that Rex was occupied at her feet under the table and wouldn't go into attack mode the second Drew approached Ally outside.

Noting that she hadn't turned the outdoor lights on, he flipped the switch as he opened the door; the last thing anyone needed was a fall in the dark.

The cool night air washed over him as he stepped outside. The misty rain that had fallen for part of the day had stopped, but the fresh smell, edged in the earthy scent from the evergreen trees in the backyard, still remained. He breathed deep and kept going, drawn to the glimmer of indefinable yet worrisome emotion he'd seen in Ally; he needed to make sure she was okay.

He found her standing clear out by the edge of the patio, looking off into the yard—presumably toward wherever Sadie sniffed around—her arms crossed over her waist, shoulders hunched.

"You cold?" he asked.

Ally whirled, pressing a hand to her chest. "Oh! You scared me to death!"

With a raise of his brows, he said, "Sorry. I turned the light on and made plenty of noise getting out here." He peered at her, noting how lovely she looked in the

glow of the patio lights and how she did indeed look chilled. "You must have been pretty wrapped up in something not to hear me coming." He took off his fleece jacket and held it out to her.

After a slight hesitation, she took the jacket and laid it over her shoulders. "Thanks." Her gaze skittered away. "Yeah, I guess my mind was somewhere else."

"Solving the world's problems?" he asked, careful to keep his tone light, noninvasive. He didn't want her to clam up on him.

She smiled crookedly. "Nothing as profound as that."

"Then what?" He cast his gaze skyward. "Looking for constellations?"

"No, but maybe I should be. The stars seem so much brighter here." She followed his gaze up, then pointed. "Is that the Little Dipper?"

He moved a bit closer, then looked in the direction she'd pointed, cocking his head, squinting. "I dunno. Maybe it's just me, but I've never actually been able to see the Little Dipper."

"You know, now that you mention it, I've never seen it, either."

Going for levity, he threw out, "I'm not even sure it really exists."

She looked at him, chuckling. "So, what? It's a giant astronomers' conspiracy?"

"Could be," he said, rubbing his chin, half joking.

"Yeah, right." She rolled her eyes.

"Hey." He lifted a shoulder. "How do you know something exists if you've never seen it?" Seemed to apply to a lot of things now that he thought about it. Such as faith.

Ally gave a pause, then a nod. "Ah. I see what you

mean." Another moment of silence. "Maybe because so many other people seem to believe in the Little Dipper you figure it must be there, somewhere, even though it seems like just a story?"

"Are those the same people who are constantly trying to convince you it exists?"

"Now that you mention it, yes," Ally replied, pointing at him. "Irritating, isn't it?"

"Yeah, especially when they tell you that you should just take their word that it's there, even though, well…" He looked up and scanned the dark, star-studded sky. "You can't actually see it with your own eyes."

"And maybe you spend some time hoping it's out there somewhere, but after a while, you give up because it seems so far out of reach?"

Suddenly, their verbal gymnastics seemed silly. "We aren't talking about the Little Dipper anymore, are we?"

"Were we ever?" she asked with a lift of her eyebrows, her soft voice just a whisper in the dark.

Drew shifted from foot to foot, then shoved his hands in his pockets, debating whether or not to ask her the obvious question or just turn around and go back in the house. His odd yet unmistakable curiosity about her won out.

"So I'm deducing that you're having a crisis of faith, too?" he asked.

"Faith?" She shook her head. "Um…no. My faith in the Lord has never wavered."

He gave her a quizzical look.

"I thought we were talking about love."

"Ah, our confusion makes some sense." He inclined his head sideways. "Faith, love. They're both hard to find."

A pause. "I'd like to believe love is out there. I mean, if I can have faith in God, I should be able to have faith in love."

He sensed more. "But?"

"But my years in foster care taught me…"

"What?" he asked, wanting, for some reason, to know what had happened to her. What, exactly, had shaped her into the strong woman standing before him.

She looked right at him, her eyes full of the painful echoes of her past. "To never believe that anyone will ever love me."

Her statement ripped a jagged hole in his heart; he understood how mercurial love was. What a crying shame that a wonderful woman like Ally had been left with such a scar, that she would be burdened with such profound doubts. At least he'd had a family who loved him. She hadn't. Suddenly, he regretted his line of questioning.

"I'm sorry." He touched her arm below her elbow. "I didn't know…well, you told me about foster care, but not the details…" He trailed off, wishing he'd stuffed his interest and kept things impersonal, wondering why he hadn't. What was it about her that intrigued him?

"Don't be sorry," she said, all sincerity, her voice as soft as the wind rustling the trees. "Everybody has stuff to deal with, right?"

He certainly admired her attitude. "Well, yeah, but it sounds as if you had it really rough growing up." Unlike him. Sure, Dad was judgmental and had high expectations. But Drew had always known that beneath the bluster, his dad loved him and Phoebe. It sounded as though Ally hadn't had that.

"Yeah, I did." She hesitated. "I've been on my own for a very long time."

Something fragile unfurled inside him, and he surprised himself by saying, "You wanna talk about it?"

Ally blinked once, seemingly taken aback by his offer, and then Sadie came waddling back before Ally could reply. Ally petted Sadie's furry head, murmuring, and in that moment, Drew's brain started functioning properly again and he realized he shouldn't be blithely offering support to Ally.

He wanted to steer clear of ties, not form them. That was the plan. The plan he wasn't following since he'd seen Ally standing there watching her home burn. Talk about dumb on his part.

Just when he'd decided to let her—and himself—off the hook and make a break for the house, she straightened and swung toward him, precluding his response.

"I guess I do," she said, looking right at him, shrugging. "Want to talk, that is. If you don't mind."

How could he say no? He'd opened the door and hadn't slammed it shut fast enough.

"Of course. I wouldn't have offered if I minded." The words rolled off his tongue automatically, and, belatedly, he realized that his statement was rock-solid true. And that hard, cold fact made him more nervous than entering a burning building. With no oxygen. No water. And no backup anywhere in sight.

Her heart skittering, Ally took a deep breath and looked at Drew standing there, the patio lights casting the angles of his face into shadow, offering one of his exceedingly broad, capable shoulders to her.

Was she crazy for confiding in him? For even letting

herself talk to him about love? Probably. But seeing the Sellers family interact had hit home how alone she felt right now—so overwhelmed, so ill-equipped to handle everything by herself. Was it such a crime to want to look to someone else for moral support, even though that wasn't usually the way she handled things like this?

She hoped not.

Sadie wandered off to sniff the lawn, and Ally took that as her cue to speak. "I don't know where to start," she said. Truer words had never been spoken.

"You said you'd been on your own for a long time?" he prompted, his voice soft and gentle. So compelling.

She nodded. "The truth is, my parents were killed in a car accident when I was eleven," she said slowly, haltingly. "Drunk driver."

Drew's face twisted. "How awful. Did they catch the drunk?"

His question made her throat tighten, and she could not for the life of her speak. Instead, she looked at the patio, her neck achingly taut, wishing Sadie would come back and interrupt. Why had Ally thought she could talk about what she'd been through, especially to Drew? The words *biggest mistake ever!* flashed in her brain like a neon sign.

Drew moved closer. "I only ask because my uncle was killed years ago by a drunk driver in a hit-and-run, and my aunt was so relieved when they found the guy and put him away."

She looked up, her neck muscles relaxing some. "Really?"

A solemn nod. "I wouldn't make up something like that."

"Of course not." She chewed her lip. Okay. Baby

steps. First, he could relate. Second, she knew enough about him to know that he was truly trying to help. Maybe she needed some of that brand of therapy. But she could only be helped if she shared her own private agony.

She pressed her quivering lips together. Drew waited patiently, his eyes never leaving her face.

Finally, she shoved out, "My mom was the drunk driver."

To his credit, he didn't gape in disgusted astonishment or blurt out any words of disbelief. He simply kept his unwavering attention on her, letting her tell the story in her own time.

She went on. "They'd been to a party, she was plastered and she drove them into a concrete overpass."

Drew reached out and took her hand, his grip warm and strong and more comforting than she ever would have imagined. Well, maybe only in her wildest dreams.

"I had no other family—both sets of grandparents were dead, no aunts or uncles still around— so I went into the foster care system." Her voice had become monotone midway through that sentence. It was a coping mechanism she'd developed—make it seem blasé and maybe it would be. Yeah, right.

"And?" he asked, squeezing her hand.

And it was awful…

"Ally?" a female voice called. "You out here?"

Ally turned in unison with Drew, still holding on to his hand with a death grip.

Phoebe stood in the open doorway leading into the house.

"Yes, I'm here."

"Drew, too?" Phoebe asked, her voice rife with what

sounded like speculation, even though she could clearly see Drew from where she stood.

"As you can see, I'm here, Phoebs." He looked at Ally and gave a little eye roll, clearly on to his sister's game. "What's up?"

"Carson has to go down to the station but he wants to talk to Ally before he leaves."

"Is she in some kind of trouble with the police?" Drew teased, pronouncing it *po*-lice.

Ally giggled, grateful for the levity.

"No, nothing like that, silly," Phoebe said, waving a hand in the air. "I think he has a job offer for Ally."

Surprise bounced through Ally, along with a dose of excitement. Another job, to go along with cleaning Myra Snow's house, which was definitely on. After an interview yesterday, Ally started tomorrow and would be cleaning Myra's house every week for the foreseeable future. "He does?" Another prayer answered. Amazing.

"Pretty sure," Phoebe said, her gaze zeroing in on Ally and Drew's clasped hands. Slowly the corners of her mouth turned up. "Although I hate to break up this little...*conversation,* you might want to come in and find out what he has in mind." She spun around and was gone.

Phoebe's knowing gaze and word emphasis knocked some sense into Ally. She was standing in the dark, holding Drew's hand, about to spill her guts.

Her brain recoiled, and she dropped Drew's hand quickly, as if it had instantly grown deadly spikes. "Um...guess I'll go in and see what's up."

He grabbed her hand. "Hey, hold up a sec."

Blinking, she silently regarded him, keeping her hand limp.

"Go talk to Carson," he said, his thumb gently rubbing the top of her hand. "But let's make a point of finishing this conversation some other time, all right?"

She chewed her lip. On the one hand, opening up to Drew beckoned like some forbidden, delicious treat hidden on a high shelf. But on the other hand, allowing herself to let someone else into her circle sent belated terror streaking through her. Her stomach knotted.

She cleared her throat, not quite sure what to say. "Okeydokey," she finally replied, trying to infuse a neutral, light tone into the expression. At the same time she pulled her hand away, remembering the pretend dangerous spikes.

With a rueful shake of her head, Ally went back into the house, whistling for Sadie. What was it about Drew that made Ally want to open up to him? His kindness? Concern? Strength? Vulnerabilities?

All of it, she decided. All of those traits combined into one fascinating, appealing man. One whom she had a feeling was going to be a challenge to keep at a distance.

Chapter Eight

Two days after Phoebe and Carson announced their engagement, Drew stopped by Mom and Dad's after work to take a look at the cable TV box. Funny how all of the electronics in the house were on the fritz lately. Matchmaking? Probably. But getting Mom to stop was a losing battle Drew didn't have the energy to fight.

He sat in his car in the driveway for a moment. Well, actually, he was here because he also wanted to talk to Ally, although if anyone had asked him to confirm that fact, he would have pleaded the fifth.

But he couldn't hide the truth from himself; she'd been on his mind almost constantly lately, and their conversation on the patio had been running nagging circles in his head. He'd deliberately stayed away for two days, not wanting to flip her—or himself—out by showing up every day.

But now…now it was time for them to finish their discussion. Hopefully, once he heard her story, he'd be able to assuage his odd curiosity and banish her from his thoughts.

He got out of the car, glad the rain had tapered off,

and headed into the house, noting on the way to the front door that his mom's annuals were finally showing some color. About time. Stuff always bloomed late in Moonlight Cove, and he was looking forward to the warmer weather in Atherton.

As soon as he stepped into the house, he could tell Mom had dinner going. The smell of roasted chicken permeated the air, and his stomach growled. Okay, so maybe he was also visiting for a meal from the best cook around.

The kitchen was empty. He snagged a few dog treats from the plastic container on the counter, keeping an eye out for Rex the Protector, and shoved them in his pocket for easy access. Couldn't hurt to be prepared if Rex got his hackles up.

Then Drew headed to the family room. Just as he moved past the doors leading to the patio, country music drifted to his ears—something about an aching, breaking heart? A few steps later, he determined the tunes were coming from outside. The back door had been left wide-open.

He stepped through and was immediately greeted by the sight of his mom, Ally and Heidi standing in a staggered line, their backs to him, with Ally up front, dancing to the music playing on a portable boom box. Ally was calling cues, and Mom and Heidi were awkwardly following along. Line dancing at its finest… or…maybe not. Sadie lay on the patio in the shade, side-sleeping.

Leaning against the doorframe, he stood unnoticed for a while, his eyes homing in on Ally. She moved with the ease and grace of a natural dancer, her body fluid and perfectly coordinated with the music. The

song seemed to bring out a sassiness in her personality that he found completely fascinating.

Suddenly she whirled around, wiggling her hips, calling out, "Turn to the left." For a second, she seemed to lose herself in the dance moves, and he couldn't take his eyes off her. But then she lifted her gaze and caught sight of him. She immediately stilled, her hands frozen in midair, her mouth slack.

"Drew!" she squeaked, her face turning pink.

Mom and Heidi, behind on the choreography, turned late. They saw him, too, and Mom waved, then she and Heidi, seemingly unembarrassed to be caught boogying on the patio like country line-dancing queens, kept going with the steps. He waved back, gave them the thumbs-up and then winked at Ally and nodded, his teasing side coming out.

"Hoo-boy, I wish I'd arrived sooner," he called, loud enough to be heard over the music. "It's not every day a guy shows up to find the patio turned into a country music dance hall."

She stared at him for a second and then turned off the music. "Are you making fun of our dance lesson?" she asked, her eyes sparkling.

He held up his hands and backed off a bit. "No, ma'am."

"Oh, I think you are." She darted a hand out and grabbed his elbow. "Teasers automatically have to dance," she announced, her grip iron-tight.

"No, they don't," he said, digging his heels in. He'd always been an embarrassingly awful dancer. No way was he going to let Ally see that. "I'll just watch."

Just then, Rex came tearing across the yard, growl-

ing menacingly. Ally instantly stepped between Drew and Rex.

Drew held a hand out to Ally. "Let me handle this."

Rex headed straight for Drew, barking, and Drew somehow managed to hastily fish one of the really smelly treats from his pocket. "Look what I have, boy," he said, holding the treat out, expecting any moment to feel Rex's teeth sink into his hand.

Rex skidded to a stop, his nose in the air.

"Yeah, looky here." Drew waved the treat in the air. "Yummy."

Rex eyed him, then zeroed in on the treat, licking his chops.

Instinctively, Drew placed the treat on his palm and held it out, preferring to keep all his fingers. Rex inched forward, closer, closer…and then he snatched the treat away, wolfing it down with gusto.

"Here." Ally held out one of the tennis balls Rex liked to chase. "Throw this for him."

Drew did so, and Rex took off like a shot across the yard and into the bushes in the far corner.

She looked at Drew. "Wow. Good work. You've got him eating out of your hand."

"Maybe," Drew replied. "He still doesn't trust me."

"He will soon," she replied. "Once he realizes what a good guy you are."

"That remains to be seen." He shifted his attention to Ally, noticing that the sun turned her eyes to a really pretty shade of green. "Where'd you learn to line dance?"

"High school gym class." She curved her lips up into a decidedly sly smile. "We made a rule that anyone who came out here had to join the lesson." She looked to Mom and Heidi. "Didn't we, ladies?"

"Sure did," Mom said without missing a beat, nodding as she took off her navy blue sweater and laid it on the railing, revealing a pink short-sleeved shirt underneath. "If we can do it, so can you, dear." She flicked the boom box off.

Sensing an impromptu alliance forming for the sole purpose of getting him to dance, he looked to the youngest conspirator, and, hence, perhaps the weak link. "Is this true, Bo-bidy?"

She blinked, then regarded Ally, who, to her credit, didn't turn and give Heidi any signal about what to say.

"Don't you want to see your uncle Drew dance?" Mom asked Heidi, apparently having no qualms about taking sides. "Hard to believe such an athletic guy has two left feet, isn't it?"

After a blank-faced pause, a slow smile bloomed on Heidi's face. "Yes, it's true," she said, nodding quickly, obviously on to the game. "That's a really important rule that no one can break."

Ally quirked an eyebrow at him. "Told you." She hitched her thumb to the patio/dance floor, and then quickly gestured to his feet with her fingers held in the shape of a pistol, as if she were shooting bullets at his feet. "It's time to dance."

"Yeah," Heidi said, mimicking Ally with her hands. "Dance."

They were ganging up on him, three determined females. Daunting. "What choice do I have with you three presenting such a united front?"

"No choice at all," Mom said wryly, her tone light as her finger hovered near the play button on the boom box. "So you might as well just agree right now."

He looked at Ally. "You're really going to make me do this?"

"You betcha," she replied, her eyes glinting with a teasing, feisty light that both exasperated and fascinated him.

He rolled a shoulder, then glanced at Heidi.

"Please, Bo-boo." She came over and grabbed his hand. "Dance with us. It's fun!" she said, tugging.

Great. He'd look like a grinch if he didn't join in. Besides, how could he say no to Heidi? Or Ally? Or Mom? He couldn't. He was caught.

"Fine, fine," he said, rolling up his sleeves. "I'll dance."

Heidi clapped her hands, jumping up and down. "Yippee!" She took her place on the patio. "This'll be so fun!"

"I agree," Ally said, her pink lips curling into a sly smile. "Especially for me."

"I can't figure out how to get this thing to work," Mom said. She jabbed at the buttons on the front of the boom box and gave a shrug. "I'm bad with electronics. You guys are going to have to handle this."

Drew followed Ally over to the table. He reached out for the boom box just as she did, their hands bumping. Shivers ran up his arm, and he pulled back with a muted intake of breath. His heart jumped.

"Be my guest," he shoved out, hoping his reaction wasn't too obvious.

"Thanks," she said, quickly pushing the buttons on the boom box. Just as deftly as she'd pushed his....

He liked it. A lot, even though he'd have to pay the price and dance in front of her. And he wanted to push back with every flirtatious bone in his body. He leaned

down so he was closer to her ear. "I'll get you for this," he whispered, careful to keep his voice light and witty so she'd get his drift.

She turned, and her liquid-green eyes met his. "I'll look forward to that."

"So will I," he replied. Probably a little too much.

An hour and a half after Ally had "taught" Drew to line dance, she somehow found herself sitting at the dining room table alone with him after she, Grace, Heidi and he had eaten a delicious dinner.

Carson had picked up Heidi to take her to soccer practice, and Grace had drifted off after the meal, saying Rex and Sadie looked like they needed a walk while the weather held.

Yeah, right. Ally had the distinct impression Grace was matchmaking. Though Ally was sure Grace had the best of intentions, she needed to let Grace know that her scheming was futile. Ally didn't want to be matched with anyone. Not even Grace's immensely appealing two-left-feet son.

Drew sipped the coffee he'd made. "Mom told me you started your job cleaning Myra Snow's house yesterday morning."

"Yep," Ally replied.

"How did it go?"

"Great. Her house isn't that big, so it only took a couple of hours, and she's paying me well and willing to give recommendations if it all works out, so I'm happy." Ecstatic, actually. "With the housecleaning gig and the babysitting gig, things are definitely looking up in the employment department."

Drew regarded her over his coffee cup, his eyes

sparkling. "Have you ever thought about teaching line dancing? Thanks for the lesson, by the way." He put his coffee cup down, revealing a crooked smile. "It was…enlightening." He picked up one cookie from a plate Grace had set on the table before she'd made her getaway.

Ally took a big drink of her own coffee. "Really?" she asked, even though, yes, it had been *very* enlightening.

As in she'd seen, up close and personal, how utterly appealing it was to watch Drew try to line dance. The cute furrows between his eyebrows. The awkward stumbles. The muttering under his breath when he couldn't get a move. It had all been so…charming. So enthralling.

So completely endearing.

She shifted in her chair. Not what she'd been going for when she'd coerced him into dancing. She still didn't know what had prompted her to do that. She hadn't realized she even possessed a flirtatious side.

It wasn't exactly comforting to know that Drew brought the coy side out in her. In fact, the notion downright terrified her. She preferred her never-flirt-because-it-could-lead-to-something-scary-that-I-won't-like side.

After a sip of coffee, he nodded. "Yes, really. It enlightened me to the reality that I'm an uncoordinated dummy when it comes to dancing," he said. "Give me a baseball or basketball to work with, and I'm fine. Even a volleyball. Or a golf ball. But my own two feet?" He shook his head, clearly chagrined. "Nope."

"Oh, come on. It wasn't that bad."

"Yeah, right." He snorted. "I looked like an idiot."

"Trust me, you didn't look dumb," she said. More like cute and real and amazingly tolerant. A lot of guys would have taken off when faced with something they didn't do well. Not Drew. "You were a good sport." Always a good thing.

"Well, thanks." Was that a blush Ally saw on his cheeks? "Somehow I just couldn't say no to Heidi."

"I noticed," Ally said. Another check in the *Things to Like about Drew* column. "You're really good with her."

"She's a good kid," he replied. "And she's had a rough go."

"How so?"

"Before she and Carson moved here from Seattle, her little brother was killed, and then her mom flipped out and took off."

Ally's chest clutched. "Oh, no." Looked as though Heidi had been to the same school of hard knocks that Ally had. Poor thing. "That's a lot for a kid her age to deal with."

Drew inclined his head to the side as he took another sip of coffee. "I'm afraid so, and yes, she's had a lot to handle. Carson moved here to start over."

"What happened to her brother?" Ally asked, feeling a kinship with Heidi that made her want to know more.

Drew didn't say anything.

"Sorry, I shouldn't have asked," Ally hurriedly added. "I didn't mean to pry. It's just that…"

"What?"

She sucked in a deep breath. "It's just that it seems like Heidi and I have a lot of things in common, and I feel for her, that's all."

He fiddled with a paper napkin on the table. "Things in common?"

Valid question. "We've both suffered...losses."

"Yes, I remember," he said, looking right at her, holding her gaze. "You lost your parents."

"Yes, I did." She dragged her gaze away and looked at the plate in front of her. And she'd lost so much more. Her childhood. Her ability to trust. A sense of family. Roots. Things she'd have to fight to ever have again, losses that had irrevocably shaped her.

Ally got her thoughts back on track. "But if you don't want to tell me what happened to Heidi's brother, I understand."

"No, it's fine. I'm sure Carson won't mind." Drew nodded definitively. "And no question I trust you."

A warm feeling spread through her, filling her up in a way she wasn't used to. "That means a lot to me." Maybe his trusting her meant too much? "Go on."

"Heidi's brother, CJ, was killed in a convenience store robbery. Carson was off duty and had taken CJ to the store for slushies." Drew visibly swallowed. "Carson saw the whole thing."

A sick chill spread through Ally, and she couldn't find words right away. "Poor Heidi. And Carson," Ally finally pushed out. "Suddenly my problems seem pretty paltry."

"It does tend to put everything in perspective, doesn't it?"

"No kidding."

"So does that mean you're willing to finish the conversation we started out on the patio the other night?"

Rats. "You haven't forgotten that, huh?"

"Nope." He quirked a brow. "Did you expect me to?"

"Not really. Hoping, maybe?"

"Why is that?"

"I'm not used to sharing." Or depending on anyone. "It doesn't come easily to me."

"Me, neither," he said. "More things in common, then."

She nodded. "Yep." Another connection. Was that good or bad? And, hey, why didn't she know the answer to that question?

Silence. She felt his gaze on her, probing, encouraging, waiting. For her to decide. Telling her that sharing was up to her.

Unable to resist his pull, she looked at him, connected with those eyes of his, saw the softness and understanding shining in them. Something melted inside her. He'd said he trusted her. And she…she trusted him. He hadn't given her any reason not to. *Yet.*

She swatted that thought aside, trying to break her pattern and have some confidence in Drew, needing to believe he was the wonderful man he seemed to be. "So, I believe you asked me how foster care was."

"I think you're right. You want to talk about it?"

Her eyes tingled and her throat tightened. Great. Why now? Was it the subject matter? Or was it the caring she saw in the man sitting across the table from her? Probably both.

She thought of Heidi. How strong she'd had to be. How she'd embraced her new life after the worst thing imaginable had happened. Surely Ally could show at least a smidgen of that strength. With God's help, as always.

"Yes." She gave him a wobbly smile. "Yes, I do want to talk about it."

A quick spark of surprise flashed in his eyes. "I've got time now," he said. Then his gaze flicked over the table scattered with used dishes, leftovers and silverware. "Want to talk while we do the dishes?"

She blinked. In the world she'd seen for most of her life, none of the men did much cleaning up. Especially unprompted. In fact, her mom hadn't cleaned much, either, since she'd spent most of her time sleeping off her daily hangover while Ally's dad had worked two jobs to make ends meet.

Drew lifted one big shoulder and started gathering plates. "Mom cooked. She shouldn't have to clean up, too."

What a considerate guy, so different from what she was used to. Refreshing. Yet…threatening, too.

She hesitated, sorely tempted to fall back on old habits that would protect her, keep her life on the narrow, safe path she'd mapped out for herself. But now that she'd spent time with the Sellers family, heard Heidi's story and seen how happy Phoebe and Carson were, how in love, Ally was beginning to wonder if closing off had left her empty and isolated. Wanting…more?

That definitely wasn't what she'd intended when she came to Moonlight Cove. But maybe it was time to do things differently. Well, some things, at least. What she could handle. After all, people talked all the time; having a personal conversation shouldn't be *that* hard. She could always edit, if necessary.

"Now is fine," she finally said. "Let's hit the kitchen and clean up." She rose and started picking up glassware, then hovered near the table while Drew headed into the kitchen with the plates in his hand.

Ally watched him go, all tall and broad-shouldered and so utterly compelling she couldn't keep her eyes off him.

Lord, since I know You're there, please help me cope if I let my guard down and Drew works his way into my heart only to leave me alone in the end.

Drew carried a stack of plates into the kitchen and set them on the counter, surprised that Ally had agreed to talk; she obviously kept a lot of stuff close to the vest, so he hadn't been sure she'd want to finish their conversation. But he was glad she had.

Something about her tugged at him, made him want to pick beneath her surface and discover what had molded her into the fascinating woman she was today. She'd obviously gone through a lot and, good or bad, he wanted to know more.

He opened the dishwasher, smothering the irritating little warning voice sounding in his head telling him that he shouldn't be so interested in Ally. With his move to Atherton coming up, the last thing he wanted to do was form a new tie in Moonlight Cove, right? So he'd just talk and satisfy his curiosity and then he'd move on with the next chapter in his life, just as he'd always intended. Easy. Or at the very least doable.

Ally followed him, her hands full of drinking glasses. Did her face look flushed?

She put the glasses on the counter next to the sink. "I'll clear the table if you want to load."

"Sure," he said, turning the faucet on. "Shouldn't take long."

They worked in companionable silence for a bit with nothing but the sound of the running water.

He took periodic peeks at Ally. Her lovely face, still slightly tinged in an appealing blush, remained otherwise inscrutable as she dried and put the dishes away.

They were supposed to talk while washing, but he found he was enjoying the silence so much he didn't want to ask any questions just yet. Sometimes quiet was better than anything.

Outside the window the setting sun tinted the clouds orange and pink as day gave way to night, time marching on. The breeze blew the tangy scent of the ocean into the house as he washed the last pot and Ally wiped the counters. All at once it hit him how much he liked just spending time with her, doing everyday things. He hadn't felt this relaxed in a very long time.

A rogue idea crashed into him. "How about we head to the beach and watch the sunset?"

Ally hung up the dish towel, then looked out the window. "Think we can make it in time?"

"If we hurry."

She grinned. "Lead the way."

They grabbed coats in the front closet—Ally wore one of Mom's—and within a minute they were out the door.

He gazed west as they walked down the driveway at a fairly fast clip. "The sun is closer to setting than I thought." Without thinking, he held his hand out. "You up for a little run?"

She gave a cute little snort as she put her small hand in his. "Are you?" she asked, her eyes glinting with an unmistakable challenge.

"Oh, definitely," he replied, liking her cheekiness. "Think you can keep up?"

She squinted sideways at him. "You up for a little challenge?"

"I'm not called Mr. Challenge for nothing."

She rolled her eyes, but she was smiling. "Well, then, you won't have a problem taking me on, Mr. Challenge."

He stopped and let go of her hand, then put his hands on his hips, raising his eyebrows in silent question.

"First one to the beach gets to choose what we talk about once the sun goes down."

"You're on," he said, already sure of what he'd want to discuss.

"On three?"

"On three," he said with a nod.

"Onetwothree!" she yelled, running the numbers together so fast he barely understood her. And then she took off toward the beach in a blur, her ponytail swaying.

He started running after her, figuring he'd just catch up and then pass her, no problem.

Except about five seconds in, he realized that she ran fast, in perfect form, her slim legs churning up the distance quite efficiently.

She looked back at him, her face glowing. "See ya there!" she said on a vibrant laugh that flitted away into the breeze coming in off the ocean.

He slammed his eyebrows together. Seemed he'd underestimated her, although he knew enough about her to realize that that move had been foolish. This woman never ceased to amaze him and, in that respect, she hadn't disappointed.

Even so, his competitive side wasn't about to let her show him up without a fight. He'd run some track in high school, so he knew how to work the pavement. Pretty much. With a deep, even breath, he focused on lengthening his stride so he could catch up with her before he left her in the dust…er, sand.

But somehow, he never managed to get any closer to her, even though he used his "kick" halfway to the beach. She ran with obvious purpose, her stride long and graceful, her shoulders straight and still. And she was *fast*. Amazingly fast.

Three-quarters of the way there, he knew he was toast. He couldn't catch her and, if anything, she was lengthening the distance between them. While he was starting to get just a bit winded—he'd thought he was in better shape—she didn't look tired at all.

She reached the beach and ran in a circle when she hit the sand, her arms in the air. In victory.

He ran up next to her. He stopped, determined not to let her see him breathe hard. He had his masculine pride. "You're a runner, aren't you?"

She gave him an impish smile. "I ran cross-country in high school. Second in State two years running."

He shook his head. "You hustled me."

"No, I did not," she replied succinctly. "I was very clear that I was up to the challenge. At no time did I indicate that I didn't know how to, um, I don't know… *run like the wind?*"

He gave her a dubious look, though she made a good point. He certainly liked this teasing side of her.

"You just assumed I wasn't fast 'cause I'm a girl," she said, throwing him a mock offended look.

"I did not think that." Not really...

"Whatever you say, Mr. Challenge." She came closer and leaned in. "Because I won fair and square," she whispered sotto voce.

Before he could reply, his gaze snagged on the orange ball of fire at her back. "Whoa, the sun is almost down." He gestured west.

She looked where he'd pointed. "Wow," she said, her face going slack before she turned back to him, her eyes glowing with what looked like incredible wonder through the wisps of hair the breeze blew around her face. "We caught a good one, didn't we?"

Stepping closer, drawn to her in an inexplicable yet undeniable way, he stared deep into her gorgeous emerald-tinted gaze. She stared back, unblinking.

His breath caught, but he managed to reply, "We sure did."

She smiled, a gentle upward tilt of her mouth that set his heart into overdrive, and then she swiveled around to look toward the ocean.

It felt so right then to take her hand in his, to touch her as they witnessed the sun sink into the horizon, on its way to the other side of the earth and back again. Golden rays slanted through holes in the clouds, shining down.

"It's as if God is there, putting on a show just for us," he said.

"You're right," she said.

He felt Ally move nearer, and it was the most natural thing in the world to let go of her hand and put his arm around her shoulder and pull her closer.

As he stood there and her sweet-smelling hair tickled

his face, it hit him that he was linked with her, perhaps in more ways than one. And, right or wrong, wise or foolish, he couldn't imagine anyone else he'd rather be with at this spectacular moment.

Chapter Nine

Ally simply could not believe she was standing on the beach with Drew's arm around her, looking at the most beautiful sunset she'd ever seen. Though she had a feeling even the most humdrum sunset would have looked good to her right now.

She sighed, snuggling closer, determined to just live in the moment for now and forget about what was safe, for once. That would mean pulling away. Being in his arms felt so right, so perfect, there was no way she was going to walk. When had she ever stood on a beach in a man's arms, feeling as if they were the only two people in the whole world? She would savor this moment, hold it all close and commit it to memory. It would be all she had of him when he left.

Drew didn't say anything for a while, and she was content in their silence. A few seagulls soared overhead, riding the breeze before they flew away, becoming nothing but black shadows disappearing into the brilliant colors of the setting sun.

His arm tightened on her shoulder. "I can't remember the last time I watched the sunset."

"Me, neither."

"Kinda sad, since I live here."

"There won't be any sunsets like this in Atherton, will there?" she said.

She felt him stiffen, and she immediately regretted her words, though she knew they just reflected the truth—Drew was leaving town, soon. There was no getting around that fact.

"Nope," he replied, his voice edged in sudden tension. "Guess that's a trade-off I'll have to make."

"Guess so," she said. "Life is all about trade-offs, isn't it?"

He pulled back and looked at her, his eyes intent. "Sounds like you've had to make a lot of them."

She glanced away, staring at another gull fighting the wind and staying in place, as if it had invisible tethers on his wings. "Yes, I have, but not by my own choice."

"Foster care?"

All she could do was nod.

"Ally, look at me."

She did as he asked, wishing all at once that she hadn't, and that she could look at him forever. So confusing…

"I know you won the race, so you don't have to have this discussion if you don't want to."

She smiled, happy he'd honor her wishes either way. But, then, that was the kind of guy he was—considerate, kind, thoughtful. "Thank you for that." She chewed on her lip. "But…maybe I need to open up a bit."

"I take it you're not used to doing that?"

"No." She let out a low sigh. "I learned early on to keep my thoughts and feelings to myself."

"I get that," he replied, gazing out at the ocean. He paused.

She waited, giving him all the time he needed to explain himself.

"I let myself lean on someone once, and it didn't turn out well."

Interest flared. "Someone you loved?"

"In college." His mouth thinned. "We were engaged, and just about the time we were going to set a date, she dumped me for an Italian exchange student."

Her chest tightened. "Oh, wow." She shook her head. "That must have really hurt."

He simply nodded. Clearly this was a sensitive subject for him.

For her, too. "That's exactly why I don't allow myself to entertain thoughts of falling in love."

"Another thing we have in common," he said softly. "You've been hurt, too."

She put her hands in her jacket pockets, feeling chilled. "Yes, foster care wasn't a good experience for me." Understatement of the century.

He turned, then touched her cheek, a warm caress that made her tummy tumble. "Tell me about it."

She swallowed, knowing she was going to have to blurt the whole story out without stopping if she were going to have any hope of getting through this discussion without breaking down. "After my parents died, I had no family and I went into foster care. My first foster father…looked at me all wrong, and he did the same thing to Sue."

Drew's eyes darkened.

She went on, quickly, as if she could somehow erase what had happened by talking fast. "Then, at the next one, my foster mom...slapped me around."

"Oh, no," he breathed, his arm gripping her shoulder.

She forced herself to go on. "Yes. I confided in my foster brother, whom I trusted, and the next day, my foster mom found out I'd said something, and she went ballistic. In the scuffle, she pushed me, and I fell and broke my wrist." She held up her right hand. "My foster brother saw the whole thing.

"The E.R. doc called the state Department of Child Services, and when they investigated, my foster mom lied and said I fell going down the stairs." Ally's eyes burned. "My foster brother backed up her lies, and since I had a record of difficult behavior on file from a few years earlier, the authorities didn't believe my story."

His jaw flexed. "What did you do?"

"I toughed it out, threatened to go back to DCS daily to keep her in line, and left the minute I turned eighteen."

He shook his head. "I am so sorry," he said, pulling her close again. "No one should have to go through that."

Her eyes burned. "Thank you."

"No wonder you keep things in. You've been betrayed by people you trusted, haven't you?"

"Story of my life." Trust wasn't something she gave easily. Or at all, really. So why now, with Drew?

His jaw tightened again, and his eyes flashed with banked fury. "I can't abide people who abuse others," he said, his lips barely moving.

"But the good news is I'm strong now, and I'm

changing the story of my life little by little. That's why I moved to Moonlight Cove. Sue, one of my foster sisters, visited her uncle, Mr. Whitley, here in Moonlight Cove once before she went into foster care, and she told me about this place. I remembered every detail, and I vowed to move here one day and start over."

"And you've done that, all on your own."

"Oh, no. Not on my own."

A crinkle formed between his eyebrows.

"Ever since Mrs. Landry, who lived next door to my parents, took me to church when I was a kid, I've had God."

Drew's face went completely still and he looked away, his jaw visibly rigid.

"What?" A thought occurred to her. "Don't you believe in God…? No, wait. Just a few minutes ago you made a comment about God's light show…."

"I believe in God," he said quietly.

"Then…what? Something's obviously bothering you."

He swung his gaze her way. "Lately my faith has been shaken."

"Why?"

"I've seen quite a few people lose the homes I sold them, seen marriages strained, families ripped apart." His eyes darkened and his face twisted. "What kind of God lets that happen to good Christians?"

"I've wondered the same thing," she said, grasping his hand.

His grip tightened. "Of course you have," he said, grimacing. "Now that we've talked, I should have realized that."

"Yeah." She swallowed. "It's no secret now what I've been through."

"Is that a bad thing?" he asked.

She lifted one shoulder. "I've always kept things to myself. It feels…weird to share stuff with other people."

"But you share stuff with God, right? You depend on Him."

"Right. I've always believed that He will be there for me, no matter what." She turned and looked at the darkening horizon, noting that the rays of the setting sun were still shining through the clouds. Yes, God was there, He was all around.

"How did you keep your faith?" Drew asked.

She thought about his question. "It's not a conscious thing." She laid a hand over her heart. "I've just always had this feeling in here that the Lord is there for me."

Drew nodded slowly, obviously absorbing what she was saying.

She went on, inspired by her own statement. "To me, faith isn't about expecting God to fix things. It's about knowing you can depend on Him for support and guidance and His wisdom when life gets tricky."

Drew put his arm around her. "Like now?"

Most especially, with him standing close, holding her, coaxing her deepest thoughts out, things she'd never told anyone. Was it that obvious how torn she was by her growing feelings for him? "Um…what do you mean?" she asked, hedging.

"You know? Because of the fire?" he said.

"Oh." She gave an awkward laugh, glad his mind was on another track. "Yeah…because of the fire." She probably sounded like a befuddled dolt. Funny how he did that to her.

"I guess I never thought about faith that way," he said. "Am I expecting too much from God?"

"I don't think you can ever expect too much," she replied. "I think you have to realize that God gives humans free will to make our own choices—"

Drew's cell phone sounded, interrupting Ally.

"One sec." He stepped sideways and held up a hand as he pulled out the phone. "Hello?" A pause. "Oh, hi, Mom." He listened for a few moments, nodding. "Okay, we'll head back right now." He pressed End, then looked at Ally. "Looks like Sadie is getting ready to have her puppies."

Ally's heart bounced. "Oh! Wow. I didn't expect that to happen quite so soon."

He grinned. "Well, the mama dog had different ideas." Out came his hand.

She took it without questioning the rightness of doing so and started walking.

With a tug, he gently stopped her. "Ally?"

Turning, she said, "Yes?"

"Thank you for being so honest with me," he said, his gaze soft yet direct. "I know sharing wasn't easy for you."

"It wasn't. But life is full of hard choices, right? You've had to make one recently, haven't you?"

"You've got that right. I agonized for years before I decided to move to Atherton," he said, echoing her thoughts. Before she could reply, he added, "Also, thank you for giving me a different perspective on my faith in God. I have a lot to think about."

"I'm glad I could help," she said. "I really think the upcoming changes to your life will be easier if you rely on God to help you through."

He inclined his head. "I'll think about that." He gestured in the general direction of Grace's house. "Let's go see Sadie and help welcome her puppies."

Though she was caught off guard by what he'd admitted, Ally managed to fall in step beside him without tripping, still holding his big, warm hand. "You're going to stay until they're born?"

"I'd like to." He tossed a questioning gaze her way. "Is that all right with you?"

Her heart soared in a way that rattled her guard even more. After a pause, she pulled herself together and slanted him a teasing smile, which was better than giving in to her wobbly knees. "I don't know. Do you have any puppy delivery experience?"

He shook his head. "No, but I helped the chief deliver a human baby once. Does that count?"

Ally's jaw fell. "You did?"

"Yep. A tourist went into labor and delivered her baby at the gas station on Main Street."

"Wow" was all she could say. When would this man quit surprising her?

"It was one of the greatest experiences of my life."

"Really?"

"Really," he said solemnly.

"Then I guess you qualify as my assistant newborn puppy nurse."

He saluted. "I'm yours for as long as you need me."

His statement had the warm and fuzzies doing crazy cartwheels round and round inside her, but only for a wonderfully clueless moment. Then reality kicked in and she came back down to earth with a resounding crash.

Drew wouldn't be around forever, and no matter

how much she was drawn to him, she couldn't afford to forget that he was leaving town—and her—behind very soon. Getting attached was a heartache waiting to happen.

Three hours after Drew left the beach with Ally, Mom's house had turned into puppy central. Now, he sat next to Ally in the whelping area she and Mom had set up in the laundry room.

Five pups had been born—three females and two males—and all of them were seemingly healthy. They were now clean and snuggled up to Sadie, making funny snuffling sounds as they tried to move blindly around.

Ally sat on the floor next to Drew, stroking Sadie's muzzle, murmuring words of encouragement. Sadie panted while she labored to deliver the sixth pup. She had been a star, bringing her babies into the world easily and then tending to them in between each puppy's arrival, just as a good mama dog should.

Ally had been a star, too, taking over the puppies' birth like a seasoned pro, even though she'd told him that everything she knew about puppy birth she'd learned online. She'd been calm, proactive and efficient. And her love for Sadie was obvious, too.

Ally clearly had a soft, compassionate soul; he'd seen tears in her eyes when they'd had to banish a curious, concerned Rex to Mom's bedroom during the delivery. Mom had stuck around to make sure everything was going smoothly, and then, pleading the onset of a cold, had joined Rex in her room and had turned in an hour ago.

During this lull, Drew couldn't help but think about

his and Ally's conversation on the beach. Her story about her time in foster care had just about killed him. She'd been through smoke and fire—literally—and that broke his heart.

And made him admire her even more. She just kept bouncing back, time and time again, not letting her hard knocks keep her down. She was one of the strongest, most resilient women he'd ever met.

Maybe that was why he'd told her about Natalie. He'd felt uncharacteristically comfortable sharing his past romantic failure. It had been surprising, but Ally brought out odd reactions in him.

He went over their conversation again, recalling her ideas on faith and God. They were brilliant, intuitive and profound, and so indicative of the kind of stalwart Christian woman she'd become, even though her life had been peppered with tragedy and crises that might crush someone less faithful. He didn't think he could be any more in awe of her than he was now. She made so much sense, and he was sure his perspective on faith would be forever altered, for the better.

Because of Ally.

In the same vein, he thought about how wonderful it had felt to have her snuggled in his arms, the flowery scent of her hair as intoxicating as any expensive perfume. He'd been physically close to other women before, sure. But something about having Ally in his embrace affected him differently. More profoundly, as if there were more than just the obvious physical attraction going on.

"Oh, here it comes," she said, interrupting his reflective train of thought. Her voice was soft and low, yet

bespoke her obvious excitement. She held out a hand. "Towel, please."

He picked up a clean towel from the pile next to him, loving being part of Ally's team. Of something that was clearly so special to her. "Here you go." Sadie had done well cleaning the pups, but Ally explained that she wanted to keep a supply of fresh towels handy in case they needed to assist.

"Thanks."

Sadie whined through her pants, and Drew could see her straining to birth the pup.

"That's it, girl," Ally said, stroking Sadie's golden head. "You can do it."

Sadie looked up at her with such love and trust in her eyes, Drew could only stare at the two of them; true devotion had never been more obvious to him.

A few moments later, a tiny, light golden puppy was born.

"Oh, boy, this one's really small," Ally said, concern etching her tone.

"The runt," Drew replied, nodding, concern tightening his gut.

Ally turned to him, her eyes wide and fearful. "Too small?"

"I don't know."

Sadie went to work cleaning the little thing, licking and nudging it with her nose. But the pup remained much too still. Ally sat frozen next to Drew, chewing on her bottom lip, her eyes glued on the scene playing out before them.

Finally, she touched him with shaking fingers. "What should we do?" Panic tinged her voice, and her eyes shone with impending tears.

He remembered something he'd seen on TV once. Without hesitation he grabbed a towel. "Sadie, girl?"

Sadie looked up at him, infinite trust shining from her dark eyes.

"Here, let me help you a bit." He tentatively reached down and laid a hand on the pup. When Sadie kept still, he slowly picked the tiny thing up and wrapped it in the towel in his hands. Then he began to gently rub the pup.

Sadie didn't take her eyes off him, yet she seemed to know he was trying to help. He kept rubbing, keeping the pup in full view; mamas could get nervous.

"Is it working?" Ally asked, her voice hushed and scratchy.

He stopped for a second and took a look. The pup was still not moving. Or breathing. "Not yet." He went back to gently stroking the pup in his hands, hoping the little thing would take a breath. Ally, he knew, would be absolutely devastated if the pup didn't survive, and her grief would be his. He was determined to save it if he could.

He heard words of prayer coming from Ally, and he joined in mentally. *Please, Lord, save this tiny thing....*

After a minute or so of rubbing, just as he thought his actions were futile, the pup shuddered and took a noisy breath, followed by the tiniest doggy whimper he'd ever heard.

Sadie nudged his hand.

"Was that...?" Ally breathed.

"Yep," he said, holding the swaddled puppy up. Joy arced through him. "It's breathing."

Ally squeezed his arm.

He looked at her, his heart surging at the pure relief shining on her face.

"Oh, thank You, God!" she said, then she gripped his arm, her touch firm and warm. "And thank you, too, Drew."

The pup squirmed in his hands, and Drew kept stroking it to encourage adequate blood flow, and to comfort it, as well. Sadie sniffed the pup intently but seemed content to let Drew hold her littlest one.

He waited with bated breath, and then, after a few minutes, the pup lifted its head and gave a minuscule yowl.

"Listen to that," Ally said, her tone laced with wonder. "What a little fighter."

He held it out to Ally. "Just like you."

She hesitated, then carefully took the puppy from him.

"If it's a girl, maybe we'll name it after you." He regarded the tiny dog. "She looks like an Ally."

Ally curved her mouth into a shaky, crooked smile. "That's the sweetest thing anybody's ever said to me."

He couldn't take his eyes off that adorable smile. "Everybody should have such a worthy namesake."

Lifting the newborn up, she took a close look at its tiny face. "You hear that, pup? He thinks I'm worthy."

"Definitely," he replied with all honesty. Just as quickly, he recalled her story, what she'd been through, how everyone in her life who mattered had made her feel unwanted. *Un*worthy. His heart cracked a little bit more, adding to the web of chinks she'd already put there.

The pup whimpered, and Ally started rubbing its back, crooning, her voice muted yet rife with a nurturing tone meant to soothe. Drew smiled and watched, enchanted by this side of Ally. By everything about

her. She was strong, kind and beautiful, both inside and out, when she could have so easily been cold and hard and bitter from the scars of her traumatic childhood.

Fury rose inside him, hot and unmistakable, and he had the sudden urge to track down everyone who'd ever hurt her and teach them a thing or two.

Then an awful thought bolted through his mind, taking his breath away.

When he left Moonlight Cove, he'd be another person who'd left her behind. Worse yet—if that were possible—suddenly the idea of leaving as he'd always planned didn't seem quite so appealing anymore.

Chapter Ten

Ally looked at her watch. 2:00 a.m. The middle of the night after a busy day. Yet she'd never felt so energized. Sure, delivering puppies was life-affirming, and, as such, revitalizing.

But she wasn't a complete head-in-the-sand idiot; she knew much of her energy and positivity was due to the man sitting next to her on the floor of Grace's laundry room–turned–canine whelping area, holding a tiny puppy as if it were the most precious thing on earth. The man who'd helped her deliver six puppies with nary a frazzled look or word. If he were this good under pressure, he'd be a great paramedic, hands-down.

Most especially, she'd noted, Drew had been so calm, so levelheaded when the runt—a female, they'd discovered—had been born. Just as Ally had been on the edge of panic, he'd taken over and saved the pup. Was there anything more wonderful than a man who could be calm under pressure and take a teensy newborn pup and literally bring it back from the brink of death?

He'd risen about a hundred notches in her estima-

tion, and he'd already been way up there before his puppy heroics. He was hovering in the stratosphere in her mind right now. And in the vicinity of her chest, too, which was, oddly, feeling both empty and full at the same time. Save a puppy, steal her heart? Could it be that effortless for him to work his way under her skin?

She shifted uneasily on the floor. Oh, boy. She was getting in over her head for sure.

"Is your back starting to hurt?" Drew asked, his brow furrowed. Amazing. He was always concerned for her, more than anyone else in her life. Ever.

Trying to act normal when little warning bombs were exploding in her brain, she stretched her neck both ways. Okay, so her back was a little tight. Not unexpected, considering they'd been down here for going on four hours. If she told him that, would he drag a chair in, or something equally as considerate?

Instead, she shook her head. "Nah. I'm tough."

"I know."

Oh, yeah. He knew her whole ugly story, 'cause she'd put it all out there. Needing a change of subject, she looked at the puppy, whom they'd named Allison after Ally's given name. "How's she doing?"

They'd tried to get her to nurse, but she wasn't mobile enough yet. Hopefully, she'd rally quickly, or an emergency call to the local vet would be in order.

Ally tried not to worry that she had no money to pay for the vet, though in a few weeks she might have enough saved up from babysitting Heidi to pay a portion of a vet bill. Nightly she thanked God for Carson's job offer, and it was certainly no chore to keep

Heidi entertained at Grace's house for a few hours after school.

"She's squirming," he replied. "Should we try to see if she'll eat again?"

"Yes, let's." Ally needed a distraction. Quick.

All the other pups had crawled over and started nursing with that instinct that all mammals had. Ally gently moved the biggest one aside, a strapping male they'd named Tank. Then, holding her breath, she watched as Drew set Allison down close to her mama, so all the little girl had to do was lift her head and eat away.

Without much thought, Ally reached out and took Drew's hand. "Let's say a silent prayer."

He stilled and then nodded. In unison, they bent their heads, and Ally asked God to save the precious, tiny puppy. She felt Drew's presence with everything in her as they prayed silently on their own, yet, somehow, as one.

Doing her best to keep focused on what mattered, Ally kept her eyes on Allison and, after a few moments, the pup sniffed around, her little eyes obviously still closed as they would be for the next few weeks. Then, nature prevailed in just the way Ally had hoped, and Allison lifted her head just a bit, rooted around and… latched on to Sadie.

Drew squeezed Ally's hand. "Looks like she knows what to do."

She nodded, then looked upward. "Thank You, God, again, for heeding our prayers."

"Amen," Drew murmured.

Ally blinked. "Are you back to talking to God?" she asked hopefully, feeling deep in her soul that Drew relying on God was a good thing.

Drew looked at her, his blue eyes intent. "Yes, and it feels…good." Without a word, he leaned over, slid his arm around her and pulled her close. "And I have you to thank for that."

She sank into his embrace, not wanting to fight it any longer. It seemed like the most natural thing in the world to lift her face. He gazed at her for a long, pulse-pounding moment, and then his head dipped and he kissed her, an ever-so-soft touch of his lips. She hung on and kissed him back, her good sense scrambled, all thoughts of keeping her guard up dashed away by the touch of Drew's lips. And so much more.

He pulled back but stayed close, and his hand came up to tenderly cup her jaw. "I didn't plan on kissing you."

"I know." She leaned in and rested her face in the space between his neck and shoulder, savoring the wonderful feeling of being close to this man. "I didn't plan on kissing you back." But she had. Without thought or hesitation.

"I'm not planning this, either," he said, lifting her face for another kiss, this one more intense than the first.

Ally felt the kiss clear down to the soles of her slipper-clad feet. At that moment it was clear that she'd made a multilevel connection with Drew, one that was deeper than any she'd ever formed before.

A dangerous bond, one that would have the power to change her life. Or topple her world.

Two days later, Mom called Drew at work from her garden-club meeting. She was beyond frantic after Dad had called her from the E.R. with complaints of chest

pains. With dread hollowing out his belly, Drew quickly told her he would meet her there.

As he jetted across town, nearly breaking the speed limit to get to the hospital, he briefly considered calling Phoebe. But she was out of town on business, and he didn't want to worry her before he knew what was up with Dad.

His hands tight on the steering wheel, Drew sped into the hospital parking lot, slammed the truck into Park in a designated E.R. space and quickly exited the vehicle.

He hurried through the drizzle to the main doors and veered left to the E.R. reception counter.

"May I help you?" a plump, gray-haired nurse in pink scrubs asked him.

"Yes. My father was admitted with chest pains."

"His name?"

"Hugh Sellers." Drew couldn't believe he was uttering his dad's name at an E.R. desk—Dad had always been as healthy as a horse and hadn't taken a sick day at work for as long as Drew could remember.

"Ah, yes," the nurse said. "Your mother arrived a few minutes ago."

The nurse pointed left to some double doors. "Go through there, and then make a right. E.R. bay 4 is halfway down on the left."

"Thank you."

Drew headed through the doors, trying not to think the worst about the situation. Maybe Dad was just overtired or stressed out. Wouldn't be surprising given what was going on between him and Mom.

Drew found E.R. bay 4. The curtain was closed, so he paused for a moment to gather his emotions and

present a calm front. He planned on being a paramedic; he needed to find a way to maintain his composure through this unexpected emergency, even if it was his own father and not a stranger lying on the bed behind the curtain.

Oddly, his mind turned to Ally then, wishing she were here beside him. Not surprising now that he thought about it. They *had* shared a knock-him-out-at-the-knees kiss just a few days ago, a kiss that hadn't been far from his mind since.

He took a deep breath and slowly released it, then grabbed the edge of the curtain and pulled it aside, steeling himself to see Dad laid out in a hospital bed.

Sure enough, Dad was there, dressed in a light blue hospital gown, a cotton blanket covering most of him. He looked pale and drawn, and suddenly...old. Dad had never looked his age, so this change was...disturbing.

Mom sat next to the bed, holding Dad's hand in her much smaller one, her brow furrowed. Interesting, since they hadn't been in the same room for weeks as far as Drew knew. She looked a bit pale, too. Not surprising, he figured, given what had happened in the past hour.

"Drew." She stood and he instantly gave her a tight bear hug.

"How're you guys doing?" he asked when she stepped back.

"I'm fine," she said, looking at Dad. "Your dad? Not so much."

Drew went over and held out his hand. Dad took it, and Drew noted how cold his dad's skin felt. "What happened?"

Dad shook his head. "I didn't sleep well, so I was

up early. I went into work to catch up on some paper-work, and I felt nauseous. And my left arm and my chest ached."

Classic heart attack precursors.

"I figured I'd picked up a stomach bug or something, so I kept working."

And classic Dad reaction.

"When Jan arrived," Dad said, "she took one look at me and asked what was wrong. I told her how I was feeling, and she said her dad had had a heart attack some years ago, so she knew the symptoms. She immediately drove me here."

Made sense; the hospital was only a mile from the Sellers Real Estate office, so that would be faster than calling 911.

"So what did the doctor say?" Drew asked.

"He's not sure, so he's ordering some tests."

"Does he think it's your heart?"

"He was being pretty cagey, but, yeah, that's the way it looks." For the first time in Drew's memory, his dad looked scared. "Possibly blockages."

Drew felt his shoulders tighten. Not exactly the best news of the day. "I'll have to be sure to thank Jan."

"Yeah, I'm thinking maybe a raise is in order."

Mom broke in. "Listen, you two, I have a feeling it's going to be a long day, so I'm going to go get some coffee." She looked at Drew. "You want some?"

"Sure, that'd be great. Thanks, Mom."

She left the room.

Dad shifted on the bed, yanking on the gown. "These things are such a pain."

Drew sat down in the chair by the head of the bed. "How do you feel now?"

"Achy," Dad said, flexing his left arm. "But the nausea is better."

Drew nodded. "That's something."

"Hope so." Dad grimaced. "Listen, son, I need to talk to you."

"What's up?" Drew sincerely hoped that his father wasn't going to give him the you-need-to-stay-here-and-not-become-a-firefighter speech again. Seemed inappropriate at a time like this, but you never knew.

Dad studied his thumbnail for a long moment. "Well, the thing is, this has knocked me for a bit of a loop."

Drew waited.

"And…well, I have a confession."

Sounded ominous. He just nodded.

"Um…I haven't been completely…forthcoming about the financial state of the business."

Drew pulled in his chin. "Okay."

"The truth is, the company is on the verge of collapsing."

Shock reverberated along Drew's spine. *"What?"*

"The real estate bubble bursting really hurt the vacation rental market," Dad said.

"I know," Drew replied, jerking a hand through his hair. Everybody knew that the real estate market had been in the cellar for a long time and that resort towns like Moonlight Cove had suffered badly. "But…I had no idea things were this bad."

"I, uh…kind of kept the true state of things under wraps," Dad said sheepishly.

Drew sagged back into his chair. "No kidding." He knew the business had taken a hit. But collapse?

"I really thought that I could turn things around with some good old-fashioned hard work."

"But…?" Drew asked, though he dreaded the expected answer.

Dad wagged his head slowly. "I can't keep up, and it's only a matter of time until I'm going to have to close up shop."

Guilt hit Drew squarely in the chest, packing a painful punch. Letting out a pent-up breath, he regarded his dad. "I wish you'd told me sooner."

"I have my pride," Dad said with a lift of his stubbly chin.

Maybe he was *too* proud. "I know, Dad, but I might have been able to help." A thought struck him. "Do you think the stress of the situation might have contributed to your…problem here? You've been working insane hours."

"Maybe," Dad said halfheartedly.

More guilt piled on Drew, until he felt as if he were drowning.

"Plus, I'm ashamed to say that one of the reasons I wanted you to stay was because I thought losing you would make the business fail even sooner." Dad looked at his hands. "I really thought you were the key."

"I didn't know I was so important to the company," Drew replied.

Dad made a face. "You accounted for over half our closed sales last year. How could you not be important?"

"You never handed out much praise."

Wincing visibly, Dad said, "I guess you're right about that. My only explanation is that I was just so caught up in what was going on the company balance sheets, I couldn't see the forest for the trees. I'm sorry."

"So much makes sense now," Drew said, rolling a

shoulder. "And I'm glad you finally told me. I never could figure out exactly why you were so against me leaving."

"Well, now you have the dirty details." Dad chewed on his cheek. "Except…there's more."

Drew blinked. "Lay it on me." No sense in delaying the truth. What good would that do?

"Your mother doesn't know about any of this."

"This just keeps getting better and better," Drew said, his stomach sinking. He rose, shaking his head.

"Our…falling-out was directly related to my work hours."

A disturbing picture was beginning to emerge. "Go on," Drew said tightly. "Just…spit it out."

"Your mother was angry about how much time I was spending at the office, and we got in an argument one night when I got home after midnight."

"Now that I think about it, I remember her making some offhand comments about her 'missing' husband a while back." Drew hadn't thought much about her remarks at the time; after all, successful real estate professionals had to work odd hours, and mom had been a real estate agent's wife for a long time. She knew the drill.

"Well, it came to a head that night, and your mom—" Dad broke off, shaking his head, his face reddening almost instantly.

Drew sensed that this was big. He reached out and took Dad's arm. "Mom what?"

Dad's jaw tightened, and so did his grip on Drew's hand, as if he were hanging on for dear life. "She actually had the gall to ask me if there was…another woman."

Drew stared, his spine stiff, his head cocked. "Come again?"

"She thought I was having an affair," Dad said, his voice a flat monotone.

"I'm...flabbergasted."

"Yeah, so was I," Dad replied. "But more than that, I was just plain wounded. What she said...well, it's left a scar that is never far from my thoughts."

Drew paced away, struggling to process this information. "So, did you tell her the truth?" He didn't for one moment think his dad had been seeing anyone else, and he wondered what had prompted Mom to think such a thing.

Dad's jaw flexed. "No. I asked her how she could believe I would do something like that, and then I walked out."

More of the picture was coming to light, and Drew suddenly had an inkling about why his mom had always been so reluctant to talk to him and Phoebe about what was going on between her and Dad. "Was that the night you moved into the apartment?"

Dad nodded stiffly.

"And you haven't talked about it since?" Drew asked, his voice rising in sheer disbelief.

"Your mom thinks I'm an adulterer, and that breaks my heart into a million jagged pieces." Dad blinked several times, and his eyes glittered. "What more is there to talk about?"

"You can tell her the truth about where you were all those nights—trying to save the business."

Dad's face crumbled. "How could she believe that about me?"

His dad's reaction landed a punch. Drew cleared

his throat. "She wasn't working with all the information, Dad—information you deliberately didn't divulge to her."

"Still doesn't excuse what she thinks."

"No, it doesn't. But you have some responsibility here, too, and you have the power to fix everything."

"I don't think I've ever been more hurt," Dad said, his voice cracking.

"You've been keeping a lot of balls in the air, haven't you?" Drew asked, more lights going off in his brain. No wonder Dad had been in such a foul mood lately, so hard to deal with. So flipped out by Drew's plans.

Dad gave a shaky nod. "Yeah, I have. And it's been really wearing on me." He gestured around. "Obviously."

Weight pressed down on Drew's shoulders. "You should have told me," he said. "Why did you hide all this from Mom and me?" Drew asked again, hoping he could eventually understand.

Dad looked ashamed. "Foolish pride. I've always been the one to keep this family going financially. I just couldn't face admitting to you guys that I'd failed."

A knot wound tight in Drew's head. "We would have understood," he replied. "Now…well, now we've got an even bigger problem on our hands. Now your health is suffering as well as your marriage."

"What should I do?" Dad asked.

"You need to come clean to Mom as soon as you can."

"I figured that's what you were going to say." Dad shook his head ruefully. "I'm such an idiot."

"I have another suggestion."

"Tell me."

"You need to pray to the Lord for help in dealing with this situation." It felt good to believe that God could help, that Drew and his family had a Higher Power to lean on when things got tough. Ally had shown him that.

Dad smiled. "When did you get so smart?"

Drew bent down and hugged him. "You taught me everything I know."

"Until now, I would have believed that." Dad's voice was husky. "Now, I'm not so sure."

Drew pulled back and saw tears on his dad's pale cheeks. Drew's own eyes burned, and a lump formed in his throat. "You're human, Dad, and your mistakes were made out of love. God knows that, and so do I. And Mom will see it, too."

"I hope you're right," Dad replied, sniffing. "I've made a mess of things, and I've held myself aloof from your mom when I should have been relying on her from the start, when I should have let our bond see us through."

"Sounds like you've learned something from this."

"Yeah, the hard way." Dad peered at him. "Are you taking notes?"

"What do you mean?"

"Phoebe told me about you and Ally."

Drew tried hard to look perplexed. "What about her?"

Dad smiled knowingly. "That you two have been spending a lot of time together lately."

"I—"

"And that you like her."

True. "She's nice, but—"

"But what?" Dad pointed at him. "Take it from me

and don't squander love. Don't hold things in." He looked around. "Look where that tack has gotten me."

Drew didn't know what to say—this was a lot to take in, given the stressful situation. Or ever, really. Plus, he wasn't sure he wanted to argue with Dad while he was lying in a hospital bed with chest pains.

Just then, an orderly arrived to ferry Dad to his tests, saving Drew from coming up with a response. After a brief conversation, the orderly unlocked the bed and started wheeling his dad out the door.

"You'll think about what I said?" Dad asked, piercing Drew with a razor-sharp gaze.

Drew nodded stiffly.

"Good," Dad said emphatically. "Because life's too short to close your eyes to love. Just grab it by the horns and thank God for bringing such a blessing into your life." His mouth trembled. "I wish I'd done that instead of trying to do everything on my own. Maybe I wouldn't be here now if I had." And then he was gone.

Drew stood alone in the dreary E.R. bay, stunned by the turn of events. And by what his dad had said. A vision of Ally rose in his mind, and right along with that a memory of holding her close, breathing in her floral perfume. His heart started thumping and suddenly he couldn't wait to see her again.

Oh, yeah, he'd be thinking about his dad's advice. In fact, he doubted he'd be pondering much else in the near future. And for a man who'd thought his path to fulfillment and happiness in Atherton was so clear, so well planned, so perfect in every way, having a diversion from the route—two of them, actually—was a complication he simply didn't want to face.

Chapter Eleven

Ally found Drew standing on the patio in the dark. "Drew? Are you all right?"

He and Grace had arrived home from the hospital just a few minutes ago, just as Ally was going to settle in with Sadie and the pups for a cuddle session. Drew had gone directly to this spot without a word, and Grace had walked to the kitchen to rustle up a late dinner, Rex following at her heels. Not surprising, really, that Grace had headed that way; Grace's way of coping with stressful events seemed to be centered around puttering in the kitchen.

Grace had called hours before to let Ally know what had happened to Hugh. Aching for all the Sellerses, Ally offered to go down there for moral support, but since she'd started watching Heidi after school and would have had to bring her, Grace told her to stay put. Carson had picked up Heidi half an hour ago.

Drew didn't turn around, just spoke, his deep voice emanating from the darkness. "Did you know my dad designed and built this whole patio himself?" His tone held a sad edge that tugged at her.

"No, I didn't." She'd finally seen Mr. Sellers in passing last night, when he'd arrived home after midnight and she'd taken Sadie out front for a potty break, but that was as far as their relationship went.

"Well, I helped, but, yeah." A pause. "He and I hauled in all the pavers, laid them all, too." He let out an audible breath. "It was a big job, and it took us weeks, working in the evenings and on weekends."

Ally stayed silent, figuring he needed to get his thoughts out, and, amazingly, she wanted to be the one he talked to.

"Now…he's sitting in a hospital bed, with three heart blockages, about to undergo an invasive procedure in the morning."

Ally moved closer and then laid a hand on Drew's arm. "It's a lot to take in, isn't it?"

Another huff. "Yeah, it is."

"But he's going to be okay?" she asked, stepping up next to him.

"Hopefully. They kept him overnight to monitor him, and then they'll do the procedure in the morning."

"Angioplasty?"

He turned and made a face. "Yeah. How did you know?"

"Remember Mrs. Landry, the lady who took me to church when I was young?"

He nodded.

"Her husband had the procedure when I was ten or so, and I walked their dogs while he recovered."

"So he was okay?" he asked, his voice alight with hope.

"I got a Christmas card from her last year, and he's

still around, driving her crazy because he refuses to wear his hearing aids."

Drew's face relaxed. "Oh, good."

"So, try not to worry, all right?"

"I don't know if that's possible." He closed his eyes. "He just looked so…old and frail, and I feel as if I could have prevented some of this."

"How?"

A significant pause. "Dad's pretty shaken up, and he told me that he thinks stress brought some of this on."

"Because of what's going on with him and your mom?"

"Partly."

"What's the other part?" she asked.

Drew rubbed his eyes. "He also told me that the business is on the brink of going under and that he's been working such long hours to save it single-handedly."

"That would be pretty stressful," she said, trying not to let her shock show, sensing Drew needed an even keel right now.

"And he hasn't told my mom what's going on."

Ally dropped her jaw. "Oh, wow." She thought for a moment. "So he's been trying to turn the business around in secret?"

"Pretty much."

"No wonder he ended up in the E.R."

"Yeah, no kidding."

She regarded him. "So…I don't get it. How could you have prevented this?"

"I'm abandoning him right when he needs me the most," he said in a husky whisper. "No wonder he's been so freaked out by my plans."

She moved around so she was facing him. "You aren't a mind reader, right?"

He simply inclined his head in agreement.

"So you cannot possibly blame yourself for this."

"Really?" he said in a tortured rasp. "I've been selfish and tuned out, focused on my own escape, my own wants and needs, and all along, my mom and dad have been in crisis."

It seemed natural to step close, so she did, slipping her arms around his taut waist, resting her cheek against his chest. "You are one of the least selfish people I know."

After a seemingly shocked pause, he wrapped his arms around her and placed his chin on the top of her head. "I don't know how I could have been so oblivious to what was going on."

His embrace brought a sense of peace to her, despite the volatile subject matter. "You have your own life," she replied. "And your parents are grown-ups. You can't take all their problems on as your own."

She felt him nod. "I have God to help me, right?"

His words made her heart glow. "And me."

He leaned back and brought both hands up to cup her face from below, his fingers warm and gentle on her jaw. "I can't tell you how much that means to me."

She hung on his gaze, and when he dipped his head to kiss her, she met him halfway. All at once, all of her painstakingly built barriers fell.

Had she lost a big chunk of her heart to the man holding her in the moonlight as if she were the most precious thing on earth?

The next morning, while his dad underwent the angioplasty, Drew stopped by the office at Dad's request

to take care of some offer paperwork that couldn't wait. Thankfully, it wasn't long before Mom called and told him that Dad had made it through the procedure with flying colors and would be in his room shortly.

Guess it was a morning of important phone calls. Just as he was heading out to his truck to make the quick drive to the hospital, Chief Jamison from the Atherton Fire Department called to tell Drew that he'd been accepted into the next Fire Academy, set to start next week! Drew had told Chief Jamison he'd have to get back to him.

How could Drew possibly leave now that he knew Sellers Real Estate was in trouble? Now that Dad had driven himself into the ground trying to save the business?

Sure, Drew wanted to go to Atherton to be a full-time firefighter; he always had. But…now? Now his dad had suffered a big setback and needed him. Drew would feel like the worst son around if he just deserted him.

Yeah, see you later, Dad. Sorry, can't help you. Gotta go do my fireman thing. Bye.

A sick feeling gripped Drew, and his hands tightened on the steering wheel. No way. He couldn't utter those words. He just couldn't. Everything had changed in just a day's time, ever since Dad had spilled his guts yesterday. From a hospital bed.

And there it was, the heartbreaking reality, which couldn't be ignored or swept aside. At least not easily. Or respectfully. And despite his and Dad's rough road lately, Drew couldn't for the life of him disrespect his father. Not after what he'd been through.

Drew turned left at Sand Dollar Avenue, something

withering up inside of him, leaving a hollow, black hole in his chest. There went his dream, for now. Oh, well. Life wasn't easy, never had been. So be it. There would be other academies. Right? He hoped so, but with the business struggling, who knew? And, frankly, the older he got, the less chance he had to stand out against younger applicants.

He parked his truck in the hospital's parking garage and sat there for a few moments, his head down, as disappointment weighed on him.

A prayer rose in his head. *Please, Lord, help me to weather this turn of events. Help me to accept this unexpected development with grace and consideration and with the wisdom to see that this is the right thing to do.*

Some of the weight lifted from him as he asked for God's help, and he mentally thanked Ally for reminding him about why he needed to reconnect with the Lord. With thoughts of her came another realization— look how gracefully she'd dealt with the setbacks that had been part and parcel of her life. If he could emulate her, even just a little bit, he'd be okay. She was an amazing woman.

With that thought providing strength—and immeasurable comfort, which he was grateful for—he went into the hospital, noting as he walked that the sun had come out after a steady morning drizzle.

When he reached the inpatient surgery waiting room, he stopped in his tracks at the unexpected sight that greeted him. Ally was there, holding up a magazine, pointing out something to his mom, who sat next to her.

Something melted inside him at the sight of Ally,

and not just because she was doing the thoughtful thing by being there for him. She was there supporting his mom, too, which somehow got to him even more.

Ally's help meant a lot—even more than he'd realized—and a big part of him wondered how well he'd be handling this whole medical crisis if not for her. Not well, probably. But he had other, more pressing matters to worry about right now. Such as a father fresh out of an invasive procedure and a mom who was estranged from her husband and had no idea why things had spun so far out of control.

"Hey," he said, joining the two women.

Mom turned and Ally stood. She wore a hot-pink fleece top with figure-hugging jeans, and she had her hair pulled back in a low, loose ponytail. She looked very pretty.

"I didn't know you were going to be here," he said.

"Do you mind?" she asked somewhat tentatively, obviously taking his statement the wrong way.

"Not at all," he replied truthfully as he slipped an arm around her shoulder, needing her steady support. In fact, he liked that she was here. More than he would have dreamed a few weeks ago. A lot had changed since Ally had come into his life.

She sighed. "Oh, good."

"Your dad is back in his room now," Mom said, raising an eyebrow, her eyes lingering on Drew and Ally. "We were waiting for you to go see him."

Drew was glad she didn't comment on his and Ally's obvious closeness. He only wanted to deal with one "crisis" at a time, and Dad's condition took precedence right now. Clearly, Mom saw that, too.

"Thanks. Let's go see him."

Mom pointed at the hall. "I'll meet you there. I have to use the ladies' room." She left the room.

"You ready?" he asked Ally, gently pulling on her shoulder.

Ally dug her heels in and hung back. "I'll wait here."

He turned. "What?" he asked, frowning. "Why?"

She crossed her arms over her abdomen. "This is a family matter."

Ah. And she didn't feel as if she were part of the family. Just as she had never felt a part of any other family. His heart just about crumbled in his chest.

He took her hand in his. "Yes, it is. And right now, you're part of this family, and I'd like you to go with me."

She bit her lip and stayed silent for a moment. "You sure your dad won't mind?"

Drew thought back to his conversation with his dad yesterday. "I'm sure."

She looked doubtful. "Well, if you're sure…"

"I am," he said, taking her hand. "Trust me, he'll be thrilled to see you." *With me*. Wow. Things had certainly changed fast.

He felt her small, soft hand in his, and his breathing gave a little hiccup. He looked at her and smiled, and she smiled back, her green eyes meeting his gaze.

"Thank you for being here for me," he said. "And for my mom." Again, he realized how much he liked having Ally by his side.

"You guys have been there for me," she replied softly. "Of course I want to do the same."

"It feels…nice to know I can lean on you."

"It does, doesn't it?"

Guess they were in the same place.

Hand in hand, they headed down the hall to Dad's room. Drew's mind swirled; huge stuff was happening. And he had a feeling that the potential changes hovering on the horizon were even bigger and more profound than he could have ever imagined. Or expected.

Was it possible to embrace them?

"Thank you for making dinner and cleaning up," Drew said to Ally as he slipped on his jacket. "Mom's exhausted after spending most of the day at the hospital."

Ally put the last plate away, trying not to stare at him, which was hard, considering that his presence seemed to fill the kitchen. Especially since their unforgettable kiss last night. She was seeing him in a whole new light. Uh-oh…

"No problem," she said, grabbing a kitchen towel. "Good thing my cooking repertoire is growing, or we'd be eating spaghetti seven nights a week."

He laughed. "That'd be okay with me as long as you served it with cookies."

She playfully flicked the towel at him. "Do you ever think about anything but cookies?"

He moved closer. "Actually, I've been thinking about our kiss quite a bit."

Swallowing, she regarded him. What was the sense of denying the truth? "Me, too," she replied. "It was quite…unexpected." Special…

"Unexpected?" He mimed stabbing himself in the chest.

"Okay, it was…wonderful."

"It was, wasn't it?" He stared, his eyes moving over

her face in a way that made her blush. "So wonderful I'd like to do it again."

Her breathing went all funny, and her knees got flimsy. "Oh, you would, would you?" she whispered, swaying toward him. "I guess that would be okay," she said, downplaying her reaction. Truthfully, her sanity had taken a hike to the next galaxy. At this point another kiss sounded like the best idea she'd heard all day.

He moved closer and his arms came up to rest on her shoulders. As if someone had shocked her, her heartbeat went haywire—

A cell phone rang.

Drew froze, wincing. His eyes slid down. "That's mine."

She nodded, squelching the desire to take his phone and chuck it out the window. "Business?"

He pulled the phone out of his pants pocket and looked at his cell. "Yup."

"Go ahead and take it."

His eyes shone with regret. "Guess I'd better." He dropped a quick yet deadly kiss on her mouth. "Don't move."

Exiting the kitchen, he put the phone to his ear and took the call. Ally sagged back against the counter, giving in to her rubbery legs, pressing a shaky hand to her lips. Wow. Even a little kiss had her feeling all mushy. Quivery. Like getting another smooch was the most important thing in her life. In the kitchen, no less!

She whirled around and looked out the window over the sink. She'd known after their kiss last night that she was in deeper than she'd ever intended. As in over her

head in a gigantic way. Romance had never been on her agenda. Not even near it.

But Drew got to her in so many ways—his goofy side, the way he interacted with Heidi, his willingness to reestablish his connection with God. He was a good, faithful man, and, frighteningly, he made her defenses crumble.

She chewed her lip as she watched a bird splash around in the bird feeder by the window. Was it such a bad thing that she liked him, a lot? Just the thought of letting him into her heart, taking that risk, dropping her guard, only to be hurt, terrified her. But then, the thought of another kiss sounded sublime. Feeling this way—so conflicted—was exhausting.

She stretched her tight neck side to side, sighing. As if she didn't already have enough to worry about. Obviously, the dog rescue was on hold, and she needed another job, yesterday. It felt as if her whole life was in limbo. Not exactly the best time to jump headfirst into Drew's arms, was it? But would it ever be the right time?

Suddenly, the bird shook and sent tiny droplets of water flying. Then, with a look up to the cloud-dotted sky, it flew, lifted by the breeze, up, up, up until it disappeared in the branches of a giant oak tree in the neighbor's yard. Looked as if it was on the way to its next adventure one yard over. Brave, wasn't it, to make that kind of a move into unknown territory? There might be cats next door. Or windows the bird might fly into. That would be bad. Disastrous.

Drew's voice broke her ominous train of thought. "I'm sorry to say, I have to go."

She turned, both relieved and disappointed. What a mess. "Real estate emergency?"

"So to speak," he replied. "An unexpected offer came in, and I need to meet the sellers at their house to discuss their counteroffer."

She forced a smile. "Go ahead."

With a sigh he took her hand.

She fought the urge to pull him close and kiss him silly.

"I wish I could stay," he said, his thumb tracing a pattern on the back of her hand.

She somehow managed to say, "Me, too. But a job's a job. Pretty soon you'll be answering fire calls in the middle of the night, right?"

Something flashed in his eyes. Doubt? Unease? "Right," he said, nodding, his face unmoving.

Something was up. She peered at him. "Have you had news from Atherton?"

He sucked in a breath. "Yes."

"And?" she asked, holding her breath just a bit. Okay, a lot.

"And I've been accepted." He looked right at her, his blue eyes pinning her in place. "Academy starts next week."

Ally blinked, trying to buy some time while her heart reacted to his news with a jolting squeeze. Then she chided herself; this news shouldn't bother her, right? She'd known all along that he was leaving.

And she'd begun to believe she could fall for him—just a bit, ha!—and remain unscathed. What a fool she'd been. The pain echoing in her heart was a warning to back away now, before the damage was lethal.

Somehow, she managed to plaster a smile on her

face. "Hey! That's great." She hoped she sounded genuine, because, really, this was what he wanted, and that should make her happy.

"Yeah, it is." He swung away, his shoulders noticeably tense. "Except I'm going to call Chief Jamison back and tell him I'm not accepting the offer."

Her heart gave a little leap. "Oh. Why not?" Surely not because of *her*...?

He rubbed his jaw. "My dad needs me. What kind of son would I be if I just took off?"

Foolish hope died. Of course she had nothing to do with his decision. Okay, no surprise there. Even so, he'd told her how much he wanted this move, and she wanted what was best for him, even if that meant he would leave her behind. "But going to Atherton is your dream," she softly said. "Are you just going to give that up?"

With bleak eyes he looked at her. "Yeah, I am."

She shook her head. This decision seemed wrong on so many levels.

"Aren't you just a little glad I'm staying?"

Her gaze flew to his. He stood there, the sunlight coming from the window shining in his face, turning his eyes into the color of chocolate caramels. He regarded her with what looked like...hope? Could that be? Again, the question arose: Was he staying, even in part, because of her?

Oh, how she wanted to hold on to that idea. But... she knew better than that. No one stayed for her. Even so, she couldn't help asking, "Would it matter if I said yes?" She deliberately held his gaze so he couldn't look away and avoid the question.

"I...don't know," he said. "Maybe."

Something deflated inside her, even though his answer was expected; she would have said the same thing. Just went to show that what the heart wanted wasn't always the best option. "Drew, neither one of us wants to depend on maybes, right?"

He tried to look away.

She caught his rough jaw. "No, don't look away. Answer honestly, okay? I think you owe me that."

Holding her gaze, he paused. "Right."

The bubble of hope in her chest deflated fully. "That's what I thought." She stepped back.

He caught her hand. His warm fingers burned. "Isn't maybe enough?"

I wish it could be. Another warning flashed bright lights in her head. "No," she replied firmly. "It's not. I'm not sure a hearty *yes* is even enough." Although, that response from him would be pretty tempting. Until her common sense prevailed. Which it would because she would make sure she held her sanity close.

"You've been wounded by all that's happened to you, haven't you?" he asked, his voice soft and husky. His hand tightened on hers. "I wish that weren't true."

Her heart twisted. All she could do was nod.

"I don't want to hurt you, too," he said.

"And I don't want you to," she whispered.

"I wouldn't ever intentionally do that," he added.

"I know," she reassured him. He was a good guy at heart. "But we both know nothing in love is certain. And that's not a risk I'm willing to take." She made an effort to sound upbeat. "Isn't it nice that we're on the same page?"

"Great," he said in a flat tone, letting go of her hand.

Yeah, fantastic. So why did it feel as if her heart was cracking into a million pieces?

Silence descended. There was nothing more to say.

"Guess I'd better get to that meeting," he finally said.

"Yep, guess you'd better," she replied, looking at a point over his shoulder, then moving back. Away. Far away. Maybe doing the best thing would be easier without those brown eyes of his penetrating her defenses like a loaded weapon.

"I'll see you later," he said. His car keys jingled as he pulled them out of his pocket.

"Sure." True, she would see him later. She was living with his parents. He'd be around a lot. She wouldn't be able to get away from him. Her stomach pitched.

He waved, and then he was gone. She walked over to the sink and looked out the window, making herself stand there and watch him back out of the driveway to hammer home what they'd just decided.

Once he was gone, to her utter horror, tears came. For a few minutes she let herself cry silently so Grace wouldn't hear. And then Ally did what she always did and pulled herself up by her bootstraps. She cut the tears off and occupied herself unloading the dishwasher.

Once every dish was put away and she'd started on the silverware, she decided that living here with Grace much longer was a really bad idea.

She needed a job to supplement the money Carson was paying her to babysit Heidi and the small amount she'd make cleaning Myra Snow's house. Quick. Quicker than she could find more housecleaning jobs. And then she could move out, away from Drew Sellers,

and start the rest of her life in Moonlight Cove, just as she'd planned. Without him.

Her heart cracked a little more, and she had a feeling it wasn't done falling apart. Nope. Not for a long time to come.

How had she let this happen when she knew so much better?

Chapter Twelve

Drew peeked around the door to his parents' bed-room. Dad was awake and reading the golf magazine Drew had left on the nightstand. He pushed the door open further. The late-afternoon sun lent just the right amount of warmth and light to the spacious room, cre-ating a cozy place for his dad to recuperate from yes-terday's surgery.

"How was your nap?" Drew asked. He and Mom had brought Dad home from the hospital earlier today, and he'd gone straight to bed to rest. He suspected Mom and Dad had talked at some point because there had been no question that Dad would recuperate here, in his own bed. Had they worked things out? Drew hoped so.

After they'd settled Dad in, Drew had headed to the office to hold down the fort there. Now he was back to give Mom a break while she "relaxed" in the kitchen whipping up who-knew-what. Honestly, he thought she should be napping herself, but she was stubborn and claimed she unwound best by preparing food. What-ever, as long as she didn't drop into an exhausted heap.

Dad looked up and grimaced. "I've had enough naps lately to last a lifetime."

Drew moved into the room. "Dr. O'Rourke said you have to take it easy."

"I'm not used to lying around."

"I know." Dad had always been active and vital, so it had to be hard to have his wings clipped like this. "But try to remember that the more you rest now, the faster you'll be back on your feet."

"Yeah, I heard the doc's instructions," Dad groused, shifting to a higher position in the bed. "I just didn't factor this little hitch into my life."

"Who does?" Drew asked, sitting in the wingchair next to the antique four-poster bed.

"Good point," Dad replied, putting the magazine down.

"How're you feeling?"

"Better than I did two days ago when this whole thing started."

"Good." Drew decided to just get the subject of Dad and Mom out in the open. "Listen, have you and Mom talked?"

Dad's face softened. "Yes."

"And?" Drew asked with bated breath, his chest tight.

"And...I took your advice and told her everything."

About time. "And?" How had Mom reacted?

Dad blinked several times, and then reached for the glass of water on the nightstand. "And she forgave me for keeping things from her."

The knot in Drew's chest unwound some. "Did forgiveness go both ways?" he asked, leaning his forearms on his knees. Dad had been devastated by Mom

thinking there might be another woman, and rightly so. That would be hard to forgive. But not impossible.

"Yes, it did," Dad said solemnly. "By keeping secrets, I had a part in her thinking the worst."

Drew sucked in a big, relieved breath, and his world felt calmer. "I'm glad to hear it."

"Me, too. Amazing how something like this makes you really see what's important." Dad cast his gaze up for just a second. "Thank you, Lord."

"God helped you, then?"

"I should have prayed to Him for guidance a long time ago."

"I'll have to remember that."

Dad took a sip of water and then regarded Drew, his eyes probing. After a long moment, he said, "Ally?"

"Yeah." Among other things. Drew cleared his throat; he had to tell his dad what was going on with his firefighting gig, even though it was a sore subject. Well…maybe not anymore, since he wasn't going to Atherton, which is what his dad had wanted all along. "And…there's more."

"I'm all ears."

"Well, I got a call yesterday, and I was accepted into the Atherton Fire Academy."

Dad's face broke into a huge grin that looked genuine enough. "That's wonderful, son."

Drew did a double take. "It is?"

"Certainly. I know this is what you wanted."

Drew stood, thrown a bit by Dad's reaction. "Thanks. But I'm not going."

Dad almost dropped his glass of water. *"What?"* He sputtered. "Why not? I thought that's what you wanted to do."

"It was, but not anymore," Drew said, turning to look out the window. Funny how the sun was shining brightly today of all days. "I see now that you need me here."

Silence.

After a long beat of time, Drew turned around.

Dad just sat there, staring at him, his jaw visibly tight.

"What? I thought you'd be happy about this," Drew said. "You wanted me to stay so badly you were even going to put out feelers about firefighting positions closer to Moonlight Cove."

"I said that, yes. But…I've changed my mind." Dad waved a hand in the air. "I've been a selfish jerk about this firefighting thing. I'm sorry about that and that I kept the true state of affairs at the office from everyone." He laughed under his breath. "Guess I need everyone's forgiveness."

"You're asking for *my* forgiveness?" Talk about a turnaround. "I figured I needed yours."

Dad scowled. "Why would you think that?"

"Because I was selfish, too."

"Stop," Dad said. "You weren't selfish at all. You were simply following your dream, and that isn't ever something to regret."

Drew shook his head. "How can I leave now, though?"

"You mean because I've spent more time in a hospital gown than regular clothes for the last few days?"

"Well, yeah."

"Oh, pshaw," Dad said with a shake of his head. "I'm going to be fine, trust me. I'm going to follow the prescribed diet, start exercising more and enjoy the com-

pany of my lovely wife." He smiled. "This was just the wake-up call I needed."

"Me, too. It's made me realize that I need to stay."

"Well, that's my fault all around, and, again, I'm sorry. But I'm not asking you to stay." He paused. "In fact, now that I think about it, you're fired."

"Excuse me?"

"You are now officially being delivered a pink slip," Dad said firmly. "Have fun in Atherton, and be sure and come visit once in a while."

Words failed Drew for a few seconds, but then a weight lifted off his heart. "Are you sure?"

"Positive, and I should have said this years ago, right about the time you graduated from college and moved back here."

"What about the business?"

"Sellers Real Estate will be just fine. Steve Carroll approached me a few months ago about merging our two businesses, and I'm taking him up on the offer."

Drew felt his jaw fall to his knees. "You're kidding." Steve Carroll owned Carroll and Company, the only other real estate firm in town, and was Dad's biggest competitor, not to mention bitterest rival. There had never been much love lost between the two men. Drew had actually been afraid of Steve when he was a kid.

"No, I'm not," Dad said firmly. "Both of the companies are struggling in the current market, and it's a good business decision to merge. Besides, Steve's younger than me and still wants to work the long hours. I can stay involved in the business, but I'll be able to cut back a bit and enjoy spending time with your mom."

Made sense, even though merging with Carroll was the last move Drew had expected his dad to make. An-

other thought occurred to him. "Have you talked to Mom about this development?"

"She's the one who suggested it."

"So she approves."

"She does," Dad replied.

More weight lifted off Drew, and excitement bubbled in his blood. Looked as if he was free to go to Atherton with nothing in Moonlight Cove keeping him here.

He shook his head, frowning.

Except Ally.

Drew's happiness came crashing down. Going to Atherton would mean leaving her behind. Suddenly, his stomach hollowed out. He recalled their conversation in the kitchen last night. Neither one of them was ready for anything serious. Yet…there was something there, something he was having a hard time denying. What was it about her that pulled at him? He couldn't get her out of his mind, and when he wasn't with her, he wanted to be. When he was with her, all he wanted to do was take her into his arms and kiss her again.

Dad's voice cut in. "Ally's really caught your attention, hasn't she?"

"How did you know?"

Dad rolled his eyes. "Your mom told me."

"I do care about her," Drew replied. "But…it's complicated."

Dad made a face. "Complicated?" He waved a hand in the air. "Only if you make it complicated. If you want it to work, it will," Dad said.

"It's not that easy."

"Sure it is," Dad replied matter-of-factly. "And coming from someone who almost lost the love of his life,

trust me, falling in love isn't about timing or anything as concrete as that."

Drew couldn't help but ask, "So what is it about?"

"It's about how you feel in here," his dad said, laying his hand over his heart. "And whether or not you can see yourself living without someone forever."

"I'm not sure I believe in forever anymore," Drew said quietly. "I thought you and Mom were forever, and look at the rough patch you've been through."

"*Patch* being the key word," Dad said. "We're fine now."

"I know, but after what happened with Natalie, and then you and Mom…well, my faith in love has been really shaken."

"I hear you, son, and I regret your mom's and my problems have had such an impact on you." Dad reached out and squeezed Drew's shoulder. "But if anything, try to view what's happened as a lesson in love prevailing, even after a lot of pain and emotional trauma."

"I'll try," Drew said. "Thanks for the new angle."

"You're welcome," Dad replied. "Speaking of new angles, have you thought about asking Ally to try dating long distance?"

Drew considered the suggestion with fresh eyes. "There's an idea." His heartbeat accelerated. Could work, but… "What if she turns me down?"

"Well, then, at least you'll know where she is with this, won't you?"

Yeah, he'd know, all right. And, frankly, Drew wasn't sure he was ready for that particular piece of information.

For Ally, could he face the answer?

* * *

The day after Ally and Drew talked in the kitchen, she returned to the Sellerses' house employed part-time. And immensely relieved.

Last night, after Drew had left, Phoebe came by to see her dad. She'd told Ally that her best friend, Molly Roderick, the owner of Bow Wow Boutique on Main Street, was looking to supplement her staff since her lone employee wanted to go part-time.

Ally had jumped at the chance of a job lead, and, luckily, Molly had been able to interview her on the fly this morning. Even more luckily, she'd hired Ally on the spot, apparently liking her experience with dogs. And, Ally was sure, Phoebe's recommendation. Molly had agreed to schedule Ally's hours around the times she babysat Heidi, and she'd also expressed keen interest in using a corner of the store to feature Ally's rescue dogs on an ongoing basis. So everything had jelled perfectly.

Now Ally had three part-time jobs, which hopefully would be enough for her to make ends meet; down the road she'd go back to her original plan to clean houses if she couldn't make it babysitting Heidi and working at Bow Wow Boutique. Next on the list was finding a rental home she could afford. She was hoping Mr. Sellers would help her with that. Drew could help her, too, of course, but she was still feeling off-kilter from their conversation yesterday and felt keeping her distance would be best. Why risk her fragile grip on self-control?

She pulled into the driveway in the sedan Grace had loaned her, and her heart sank, yet, oddly, perked up at the same time. Great. Drew's truck sat in the drive-

way. He was here, undoubtedly visiting his dad. So much for distance.

She parked Grace's car in the garage and then headed into the house. Maybe she could just sneak in, go to her room and miss seeing him. Except she needed to stop and check on Sadie and the puppies. Their space was due for a cleaning.

Steeling herself to see him—she'd deal, as always—she put the car keys on the hook in the kitchen and headed for the laundry room where Sadie and the pups rested.

Her heart just about exploded when she saw Drew sitting smack-dab in the middle of the whole family of dogs, holding Allison on his chest. Sadie lay on her side, nursing the pups, her head on Drew's knee, her eyes closed in sheer doggy bliss. Drew's hair was attractively mussed, and the blue shirt he wore hugged his broad shoulders.

What a scene! Handsome man, mama dog and puppies, all cozy and relaxed. Ally had the urge to step right in and plop herself down next to the yummy guy, put her head on his shoulder and stay awhile.

Except she was supposed to be keeping her distance from him. Yeah, that was going great so far.

"Hey," he said softly. "I couldn't resist stopping here for a while to see how this little gal is doing," he said, holding up the tiniest pup.

She gave a little howl of distress, obviously wanting her soft, warm place back on his chest.

Ally knew the feeling. Boy, did she.

"Oh, don't worry, puppy," he crooned as he quickly put her back down in her wonderful spot, rubbing her head. "I'll stay as long as you need me."

His words echoed through Ally like an explosion. *As long as you need me.* For the puppy, sure. But for her?

Even so, Ally's chest expanded as she watched him comfort the puppy, so gentle and caring. So… wonderful.

Somehow, she found her voice. "Hey. Yeah, I was just stopping to check on them, too."

He smiled, then shifted the puppy up so she was snuggled under his chin. "They're doing great," he said. "You've done a wonderful job here."

His praise made her face warm in a very nice way. "Thanks. Though it's hardly work when I get to spend time with cute puppies," she said.

"True. They are adorable." He gestured to the floor with his free hand. "I went ahead and changed the papers."

He was so thoughtful. Overwhelmingly so. "Thanks." She licked her lips. Escape. She needed to escape. "Well, since things seem to be under control here, I'll just head to my room." A thought occurred to her. "Where's Rex?"

"Mom took him on a walk."

"Oh. Great."

"He actually let me in the house without attacking."

"He's making progress, then."

"Yep." Drew regarded her intently. "Mom told me you went to a job interview with Molly at Bow Wow Boutique."

Ally nodded and beamed. "I got the job. And Molly is interested in featuring the dogs I rescue in her store."

After an odd pause, he said, "Oh. That's good. I know that's what you wanted." He cleared his throat. "Listen, can we talk? I have some…news."

She lifted her brow. "Okay." Clearly he had something on his mind. So much for her escape.

He put the puppy down next to Sadie so she could nurse. "I'll come out there, if you don't mind." He looked back to the pup. "As long as she's okay..."

He was a man of his word. "Sure," she said, fighting the urge to chew on a nail.

When it was clear the puppy was settled and happy, he stood and made his way out of the puppy den.

Ally scuffled back as he stepped over the gate across the doorway, noticing, as she always did, how good he looked in his dark blue dress pants and light blue shirt, open at the collar, no tie anywhere in sight. Wow. She could stare at him all day.

"How's your dad?" she asked.

"He's doing great. Especially since he and my mom are back together."

"I noticed," Ally replied. "He's back sleeping in their room, and she's been spending almost every free moment in there with him. They even watched a movie together late last night. I heard them laughing." It had been comforting for her to hear grown-ups in the next room who weren't fighting. "I also had breakfast with him this morning. He's a very nice man."

A brilliant smile lit Drew's face. "Good. I was worried about them for a while, but now...well, I can relax."

"I guess some people manage to make their way back to love no matter what." Ally mentally winced. What had possessed her to say that? Was she looking for a discussion about love?

He gave her a disconcertingly direct gaze. "I guess so," he said in a very, very soft voice that disarmed her. What else was new? "Kind of gives me hope."

"Really?" she said in a strangled tone. Oh, boy. What was on his mind? Needing air, she said, "Let's go out on the patio."

Once they were there, she turned to him, careful to keep a distance, though she couldn't seem to manage that any other time. "So, what's up?"

He took a large breath, the kind someone takes when he's gearing up to deliver questionable news.

"I talked to my dad, and he fired me," Drew said.

Ally frowned. "He fired you? Why?"

"So I would take the job in Atherton."

"Ah." Now she saw where this was headed. "So… you're going?"

He slowly nodded. "I am. I really felt as if I couldn't leave my dad, but he's planning on merging the company with another local real estate firm, so there's nothing keeping me here anymore. I called Chief Jamison and accepted the offer."

Ally's heart twisted, and she hated the pain radiating from her chest into the rest of her body. *I should have expected this.* But she hadn't, not really. Deep down, she'd believed him when he'd said he was staying. Foolish move, girl. When would she learn?

Right now. No one stayed for her.

Do. Not. Forget. That. Ever.

In the here and now, she reminded herself that he wanted this, so she wanted it for him. Well, most of her, anyway. Now that she knew he was leaving, she saw that the rest of her had wanted him to stay.

With effort, she plastered a smile on her face. "I'm glad it all worked out," she said in a remarkably even, normal-sounding voice. Good acting.

"Me, too," he replied. "It's a relief to have everything figured out."

"I'm sure it is," she said. When would she have the same thing? Soon. She was so close…

He paused for a second, shifting. "Listen, about that, I had something I wanted to discuss with you."

"Okay." What was on his mind now?

He looked out over the yard for a second, his brow furrowed. "I know you've been hurt. I have, too. But I think we might have something worth holding on to."

"Holding on to?"

"Yes." He took her hand in his. "Ever since I met you, the one bad thing about leaving Moonlight Cove was leaving you."

"Really?" she squeaked out.

"Really. You're a wonderful woman, Ally," he told her, squeezing her hand. "You're kind, strong, and I really like being with you."

She swallowed. "I like being with you, too," she said softly, because it was true.

He smiled, happiness shining in his eyes. "Then would you consider dating long-distance?"

Giddiness bounced through her. She pressed a hand to her breastbone, a smile pulling at her lips. Oh, how very tempting….

But, no. *No.* Her smile died. She looked at him, standing expectantly, his eyes boring into her, waiting for her answer. A lump grew in her throat and her eyes burned. She had to stay the course.

"I saw the beginnings of a smile," he said, his words slicing the silence like a knife. "But not the end of one. Not exactly a good sign."

Correct. And she owed him the truth when he was

putting himself on the line. "You're leaving, and…a lot of people in my life have left and…" She trailed off as her throat clogged.

He nodded. "I get what you're saying. Relationships are risky. But I'm willing to try if you are."

Uncertainty flooded her, filling her up so full her eyes burned. He was asking too much. "I can't." Tears spilled over and she swiped at them. "I'm sorry, I just can't."

"Not even for a chance at happiness?"

She swallowed. She could only shake her head.

His face stiffened, and he took a step back, his eyes going blank as his shields went up. "Okay, I understand. Just thought I'd ask, even though it was a long shot."

"I'm sorry," she said inanely. "It's not enough, and I can't let myself take the risk."

"Risk." He snorted.

"You risked a lot by asking me, didn't you?"

He nodded. "But I had to know one way or another before I moved on."

Moved on. Without her. Because that was the way it had to be. The way she wanted it. Right? Though the rock in her gut told her the question was both right and wrong. She'd need to get over that if she had any hope of getting through this unscathed.

She simply nodded back, unsure of what to say. Besides, if she spoke, she'd full-out cry, and she didn't want that right now.

"Well, I guess that's it," he said.

"Guess so," she said in a husky voice. You'd think she'd be better at goodbyes by now after having so many forced on her. But, apparently not.

"Okay. I'll go now." He touched her cheek before

she could back away. "I was hoping things could be different."

"I've been hoping that my whole life," she whispered, fighting the urge to nuzzle his hand. "But I've learned that things are what they are, and I can't change that."

Without another word, he turned. She looked away and watched a bird fly into the yard and land on a branch of a maple tree. She stared at that bird rather than watch Drew walk out of her life, even though she should force herself to observe every step he took. This was what she'd chosen, what she had to face.

And when she looked back through her tears, he was gone. And so, she feared, was her heart.

Chapter Thirteen

"Don't you think you should be smiling more at your own going-away party?" Carson asked Drew, handing him a glass of Drew's mom's famous Party Punch.

Drew took the fruity drink. "I'm smiling." He pressed his mouth into a stiff smile. "See?"

"That's the sorriest excuse for a smile I've ever seen," Carson replied with a rueful smile and a shake of his head.

"I agree." Seth Graham, Drew's best friend, joined them. "Who died?"

Oh, man. These two in-love-and-loving-it guys were going to gang up on Drew for sure; ever since Seth had fallen for and married Kim Hampton, and Carson had gone head over heels for Phoebe, they had been love advocates of the highest order.

So…maybe he should ask for their advice. He really needed to talk about what had happened with Ally last week. He sure wasn't dealing with the situation well on his own. Sleep had been elusive, and when he finally had drifted off in the dead of night, Ally haunted his dreams. More significantly, his appetite was nonexis-

tent. Honestly, it felt as if he had a hollow space inside him that made him feel empty yet full at the same time. So much so that he had no desire to eat.

"No one died. It's just that…" He trailed off when he saw Ally walk out on the patio, animatedly talking to Heidi. The sun glinted off Ally's golden hair, and her ready smile lit up her face in a way that took his breath away. He heard her laugh at something Heidi said, and the lilting sound made his heart go bumpitty-bump.

Seth nudged Drew's shoulder. "Looks like the pretty houseguest has caught your attention."

"More like his heart," Carson added. "Word on the street is that they've been spending a lot of time together since she moved in here."

"Yeah, I heard that, too." Seth gave him an inquiring stare. "What's the real dirt?"

Drew rolled a shoulder. What was the sense in lying to them, or to himself? "Okay, so I like her."

"Then what's the problem?" Carson asked.

Drew scowled at him. "Do you really have to ask that? I seem to remember how much trouble you had admitting your feelings for Phoebe." He turned to Seth. "And you fought your feelings for Kim with everything in you from the moment you two met in the ocean that day." Seth had rescued Kim from a riptide while at a church singles' group outing at Moonlight Cove Beach, and the rest was history. Seth had become a wonderful dad to Kim's seven-year-old son, and now they had a baby on the way and were the happiest couple on earth. Well, except maybe for Carson and Phoebe.

Drew wanted that kind of happiness, he realized. He wanted what these two men had. But it was too late.

Carson held up his hands. "Okay, okay, we get it. Relationships are intimidating."

"Frightening," Seth said.

"Complicated," Drew added.

Carson and Seth nodded their agreement.

"So what am I going to do?" Drew muttered.

"Have you told her how you feel?" Seth questioned.

Carson piped in. "Good idea."

"I asked her to try the long-distance thing," Drew told them.

"Really?" Carson whistled. "That's a start."

"Yeah, but maybe not enough," Seth put in.

"No kidding." Drew shook his head. "She turned me down."

Carson winced. "Ouch."

"Yep," Drew replied. "She said she couldn't take the risk and that's that."

"All well and good," Seth said. "But did you tell her you love her?"

Something twisted in Drew. "No." He swiped a hand through his hair. "I wasn't sure I did love her."

Carson hit him with a direct stare. "But now?"

Drew looked over at Ally where she sat with Phoebe and Heidi at the patio table. Just the sight of her made him happy. Every moment they were apart felt like torture. Did that mean he loved her? "Now…I haven't slept, I'm not eating and I can't stop wanting to be with her."

"Yeah, I know that feeling," Seth said with a twist of his lips. "Sounds like love."

Carson nodded his agreement. "I agree. You've got it bad."

Drew's stomach pitched as uncertainty jabbed holes

in his confidence. "No, I don't think I do." He took a big swig of punch, then immediately regretted it. Too sweet. "And she's on the same page, so it's all good." The words burned.

Seth and Carson gave each other doubting glances.

"No, really, guys. This is all working out fine."

Carson shook his head. "You're lying to yourself, man."

"Yep, you definitely are," Seth added.

"Why would I do that?" Drew asked, then regretted the question. He didn't need these guys picking his motivations apart, building doubts in his mind, though he refused to consider why.

"Um…to protect yourself?" Carson said as if it were the most obvious thing in the world. Which it was.

Drew waved a hand in the air. "You're way off base. Sure, I like Ally. But I don't love her, all right?" His heart ripped as he said those words, but he ignored the tearing sensation. No sense in asking for trouble, especially since Ally wanted it this way. He'd make a clean break, move to Atherton as he'd always planned, and soon she'd be nothing more than a nice memory.

"Whatever," Seth said. "But I think you're making excuses."

Maybe. But at this point, it was the best decision all around. For both him and Ally. And as soon as he faced that reality, the sooner he could move on with his life in Atherton.

He only hoped he'd be as happy as he'd always imagined; there was no turning back now, no second chance.

Chapter Fourteen

Drew stowed the last of his stuff in the truck bed, checking to make sure he hadn't missed anything he'd had stored in his parents' garage. Methodically, he covered the load with a tarp to protect it from the rain, which had been falling all morning, and then tied the tarp in place. He jerked on the bungee cords to be sure the tarp was going to hold during the three-hour drive to Atherton.

He stood back. Okay. He was packed and ready to go. Nothing more to do. His new life stretched out before him, all shiny and pretty and exactly the way he wanted it.

Except…he felt blah and…well, numb, as if he were facing an unpleasant chore, rather than the beginning of his dream come true.

Truthfully, it felt as if his heart had been beaten up and was in critical condition.

So much for moving on.

He laid his forearms on the side of the truck bed and bowed his head. *Lord, I need Your help to follow my*

path, to do what I've wanted to do for as long as I can
remember, and to accept that this is what's best for me.

"You okay, son?"

Drew said a quick *Amen* and then turned and looked
at Dad. He was recovering well from his surgery, and it
was good to see him up and around, acting like himself.

"Fine, Dad." Drew didn't want to discuss his loss
of Ally; the wound was too fresh. Too tender to pick
apart. Maybe someday it would be less painful. He
could only hope.

Dad studied his face. "Have you said goodbye to
Ally?"

"Last night," Drew replied succinctly, hoping Dad
would drop the subject.

"And the puppies?"

Drew cleared his throat. Those puppies—the runt
in particular—were a brutal reminder of Ally, of her
heart and soul and everything she held dear. "I saw
them last night, too."

Dad studied him for a long, uncomfortable moment.
"I talked to Seth at your party."

Oh, boy. Not good. "Yes?" Drew said tightly.

"And he told me you're sticking your head in the
sand about you and Ally."

"Seth can't keep a secret to save his life."

"Did you tell him to keep it a secret?"

"Well, no." Drew grimaced. "But I wish I had."

Dad waved a hand in the air. "Too late. He spilled,
and I want to know why you didn't fight for her."

"She doesn't want me to fight. She doesn't want to
take a chance on us." He winced inwardly but did his
best to disregard the stabbing pain in the vicinity of
his heart.

"Oh, pshaw," Dad replied, twisting his lips into a scowl. "I talked to her at breakfast yesterday, and her eyes lit up when she talked about you. She cares about you."

Drew's hopes crested, but he ruthlessly yanked them down and stomped on them. "What do you want me to do? Grab her by the hair, caveman-style, and demand that she date me from three hours away?"

Dad laughed. "I'd like to see you try."

"Yeah, right," Drew exclaimed ruefully. "Ally isn't exactly the kind of woman who'd allow that."

"She likes to stand on her own, then?" Dad asked, his one eyebrow cocked up.

"Yep, she does." It was one of the things Drew loved most about her—her independent spirit and backbone. And so many other things he'd miss.

"So you're just going to drive away and leave her behind without a battle?" Dad shook his head. "Seems pretty final to me."

Final. Drew closed his eyes briefly, gathering his strength to do what had to be done. What Ally wanted. What he wanted, too. "Yes. It's what she wants, so please, just let this go." It was too much to deal with. Too much to assimilate. Too great a risk to take for a shaky outcome he couldn't be sure of. "Ally won't ever love me, end of story."

"I'd like to let it go," Dad said softly, "but I've been alone because of my own stubbornness, and I regret that with everything in me." He laid a firm hand on Drew's shoulder. "Sometimes we all just need to have a little faith."

Drew didn't know what to say to that. How could he have faith in love when Ally didn't seem to have

any? "You're right, Dad. And I have faith that going to Atherton is the right path."

"Does it have to be either/or?"

"According to Ally, it does." Drew swallowed. "I've already made my decision, and I don't want to second-guess myself."

Dad inclined his head to the side in grudging acquiescence. "All right. I hear you. I only hope you don't regret walking away."

"So do I, Dad. So do I."

"So I hear Drew left town earlier today."

Ally looked at Molly from where she was straightening the squeaky toy shelf at Bow Wow Boutique. She'd started her first shift a few hours ago and, frankly, was grateful for the distraction of working.

Anything was better than thinking about Drew.

"Yes, he did," she said, her throat tightening. She'd stood at the Sellerses' kitchen window and forced herself to watch him drive away, as if seeing him leave would somehow make everything peachy. Rosy. Right as the rain that had started falling that morning.

Ha. Talk about the best-laid plans going up in flames. Instead, nothing was anywhere close to peachy, the rain had turned into a downpour, and she'd gone to her room and had a good long cry. And then she'd cried some more.

She was going to miss him. More than she'd thought possible just a month ago. Guess that was the breaks for letting him close to her heart.

Molly flipped her red curls over her shoulder as she wiped the front display case an enthusiastic boxer

named Bo had slobbered up. "How do you feel about that?"

Ally furrowed her brow, wondering how to respond. She wasn't keen on dissecting her reaction to Drew's departure; it would be easier to forget him without rehashing. And forget him she would. Eventually. She had to. "Um…why do you ask?" she replied, hoping to deflect Molly's interest.

"Well, it's obvious that you've been crying—"

"It is?" Ally exclaimed, her hands going to her cheeks. She'd done everything she could to get rid of any traces of her crying jag, including a cold compress and more cover-up than she usually wore. Guess she hadn't done a very good job. Then again, it had been a crying jag of epic proportions.

"Well, yes." Molly gave her a look tinged with sympathy. "Don't worry about it, though. I know how hard it is to watch someone important leave." She quirked her lips. "I'm pretty sure I bawled like a baby when Grant left town to go back to Seattle."

Ah. So Molly's look had been edged with empathy. She clearly understood what Ally was going through. Ally bit her lip, her usual inclination to handle things on her own at war with desperately wanting to talk to someone about the emotional roller coaster she'd been riding lately, thanks to a wonderful man named Drew.

Before she could respond, Molly came over and softly said, "You wanna talk about it?"

Ally's eyes burned. "Um…I'm not really a talker." Until Drew had come along. With him, she'd opened up. What a mistake. Hindsight was like that, though.

"But?"

"But…" Ally slumped her shoulders, feeling her will

to stand on her own crumble. "I'm having a hard time dealing with all this."

"Do you have feelings for him?"

"I don't want to," Ally said, hedging.

Molly smiled knowingly. "But you do, right?"

"Possibly," Ally whispered, wincing as the words came out. This wasn't what she wanted. Caring about someone was brutal when it ended.

"And I'm going to take a wild guess and say that's a bad thing in your mind, right?"

Ally nodded as she got to her feet. Molly understood. "I don't want to care for him. I've fought it all along, and I was telling myself things were fine."

"I was there once," Molly said with a nod. She gestured for Ally to follow her to the back room. "I fought falling in love with Grant for a long time."

"You did?" Ally said, trotting along behind her.

"Oh, yeah." Molly let out a rueful chuckle. "I was so, so scared to let myself love him, and I was so determined to protect my heart."

Ally trailed Molly into the back room. "Sounds familiar."

Molly got a couple bottles of water out of the mini-fridge next to her desk. "I know. I can see you fighting your attraction to him with everything you have." She handed one of the bottles of water to Ally.

Ally removed the plastic lid with a twist of her fingers. "Is it that obvious?"

"I watched you two at his going-away party. He couldn't take his eyes off you."

Ally's cheeks warmed. "Really?"

"Really. And I'm pretty sure I saw you watching him quite a lot, too."

Busted. "Maybe." Her eyes had been drawn to him often. As in every minute. She screwed the lid back on her bottle of water, wishing she could twist her feelings back in their proper place as easily.

Molly gave her a look full of doubt. "No maybe about it, honey. You're hung up on him, and you know it."

Ally sucked in a fresh breath and let it out. "So... what if I am? I'm thinking that maybe now that he's gone—you know, out of sight, out of mind?—I'll get un–hung up and I'll be able to move on with my life the way I had planned all along." She gave Molly a hopeful look. "Maybe this is just a bump in the road."

Molly took a sip of water. "Yeah, that's what I thought, too, after Grant left." She laughed softly.

"And?" Ally asked with bated breath, wanting to both hear the answer and run away at the same time. Although, since Molly and Grant were now happily married, the answer was a given.

"And trying to forget Grant just because he was gone didn't work," Molly said gently, as if she didn't want to break the news to Ally.

Anxiety knotted inside Ally. "Not ever?" she uttered, widening her eyes, realizing too late that she'd asked another redundant question. Okay. Maybe she needed to hear the cold, hard truth from Molly. Although, the prospect of facing reality scared Ally more than anything she'd ever come up against.

"'Fraid not." Molly set her bottle of water down. "I've learned that love is undeniable and enduring, and it doesn't just go poof and disappear, even with distance."

Ally just stared at Molly, shaking her head, her

throat frozen with panic. The bottle of water slipped from her hands and landed with a *thunk* on the floor.

Without missing a beat, Molly picked up the bottle and handed it back to Ally. "And if you ask Grant, he'd say the same thing. We only lasted three weeks apart before we both gave in to our feelings."

The knot of anxiety throbbing inside Ally spread its tentacles outward, tightening every muscle in her upper body while making her legs feel like overcooked noodles. This was not what the protective, love-phobic side of her wanted to hear, though she didn't blame Molly for being honest. She knew she was just trying to help.

The bells over the door to the store jangled, heralding the arrival of a customer.

"I'll get that," Molly said, her green eyes soft with understanding. She pushed her rolling desk chair closer to Ally. "You look like you need to sit down."

Ally nodded. "I think you're right." She gave in to her shaking legs and sank into the chair as Molly left the room. As Ally sat there, her thoughts humming, she couldn't help but think about what Molly had said.

Love is undeniable and enduring, and it doesn't just go poof and disappear, even with distance.

Profound words, certainly. And Ally believed the sentiment at the core of Molly's statement. But did any of this apply to Ally?

On the heels of that thought, a stunning question ricocheted through her consciousness. Was she in such a funk because she'd fallen in love with Drew? Or was she simply caught up in how kind he'd been to her, how he'd made her feel special? Important. Worthy. Things she'd never felt before.

Confusion spread through her, so she fell back on

the familiar. She pressed her hands together in front of her and a prayerful question rose from her lips. "God, I know You're listening. Please, help me. How am I ever going to figure this out?"

Just as she uttered the last word, Molly came tearing into the back room. "Ally, Grace just called my cell phone." Grace, bless her gracious soul, was keeping an eye on Sadie, the puppies and Rex while Ally worked.

Ally got to her feet, her neck prickling. "What did she want?"

"Rex escaped from the backyard," Molly said, her voice tinged with obvious concern. Molly was a dog lover and had two miniature schnauzers she doted on.

Ally's stomach dropped and panic tightened her shoulders and cut off her breath. "Did she find him?"

Molly shook her head. "No. Rex is missing, Ally. There's been no sign of him, and Grace is frantic with worry."

Just as Drew finished eating his breakfast in his new apartment in Atherton, his cell phone rang. He set his cereal bowl in the sink and grabbed his cell from the counter, glancing at the caller ID. Mom.

He smiled; he'd left Moonlight Cove less than twenty-four hours ago, and she was already checking in. Though now that he thought about it, she'd managed to hold off calling for a whole three-quarters of a day. Once a mom, always a mom. Or so he'd been told. By her.

He pushed Talk. "Hey, Mom."

"Hi, honey." A sniff and then a pause. "How are things going?"

"Pretty well," he replied, careful to make sure he sounded upbeat.

Actually, though, the hollow feeling he'd noticed when he'd been packing his truck had persisted. Maybe even become worse the farther he'd driven from Moonlight Cove. And he hadn't slept at all last night, which he'd tried to attribute to nerves over his upcoming first day at Academy, somewhere around 3:00 a.m., but was actually, he knew, more about leaving Ally behind than anything else.

He could only hope time and distance would remedy the burning ache that had rooted in his chest for the past few days, ever since Ally had told him she never wanted to fall in love.

"Good. Good," Mom replied in a scratchy voice. She then went quiet.

Silence stretched out over the phone line. Odd. Mom was never at a loss for words. "How's Dad?" Drew asked.

Another sniff. "Fine."

"Do you have a cold?"

"No."

He frowned. A one-word answer. Highly unusual. "Mom, is something…wrong?"

A sob reverberated in his ear.

Alarm screeched through him. "Mom?" He switched the phone to his other ear and gripped the device until his knuckles ached. "Did something happen to Dad?"

"Oh, Drew. It's so awful. Rex is missing!"

Drew closed his eyes briefly, shaking his head, dread pulling at him. "What happened?"

"I was taking care of him, Sadie and the puppies

while Ally was at work, and—" her voice broke "—and Rex dug under the fence and ran off."

"When did this happen?" Drew drilled out.

"Yesterday afternoon, not long after you left," Mom said, her voice cracking again.

"He's been missing since yesterday?" he barked. Ally had to be beyond frantic; she loved that dog. "Why didn't anyone call me?"

"Ally wouldn't let us."

He frowned. "Why not?"

"She said she didn't want to distract you."

That sounded like Ally, always wanting to spare others distress, always wanting to handle things on her own. "But you called anyway?"

"I figured you'd want to know."

"You have that right." He swiped a hand over his jaw. "So there's been no sign of him?"

"No sign, and we looked for him all night."

Oh, man. Not good. "How's Ally doing?"

"Not well at all," Mom responded. "She's frantic, of course, and hasn't stopped looking to eat or sleep. At this rate, she's going to collapse in exhaustion before nightfall."

Concern blasted through him, setting his already stretched nerves on a hard edge.

Mom went on. "I'm worried about her, Drew. Really worried. She loves that dog with everything in her, and she's going to be devastated if we don't find him."

He had to go to Ally, had to make sure she was okay. He needed to be there for her, even though she would never ask for his help.

"I'm coming home," he said.

"Doesn't Academy start today?"

He headed over to the single bedroom to search for his keys. "Yeah, it does. But Ally's more important."

Mom was silent for a long moment. "Oh, Drew. You love her a lot, don't you?" she asked in a hushed voice.

"I care about her, Mom," he said honestly. "But I'm not in love with her."

"Well, I think she loves you."

Hope soared, but he pounded it down as he found the jeans he'd worn yesterday and dug his keys out of the pocket. "I don't think so, Mom."

"Why do you say that?"

"Because she told me she never wants to fall in love."

"And you believed her?"

He grabbed a sweatshirt from the top of the pile of clothes he hadn't put away yet. "Why wouldn't I?"

"Maybe because you have faith in love and in Ally?"

He froze, her words reverberating through him, then recovered. "I'm not sure that's enough."

"Of course it is. You just don't know it yet."

"I don't agree with you," he replied. "But right now, I don't have time to discuss the matter. I just have to get back to Moonlight Cove and help search for Rex."

"What about Academy?"

"There will be other academies," he replied, hoping his words proved true. He'd deal with that when the time came.

"But there won't be another Ally, will there?"

His throat clogged. "No, there won't," he said thickly, heading out to the living room. She was one of a kind.

"So, why aren't you willing to take a risk for love?"

He felt the beginnings of a headache and hoped he'd

remembered to pack some ibuprofen. "Mom, I have to go so I can get home and help look for Rex." Nothing more. No love, no risk. Good or bad, right or wrong, he'd deal with that reality.

What other choice did he have?

Chapter Fifteen

Ally sat at the Sellerses' kitchen table and stared at the fried-egg sandwich Grace had kindly made for her. Ally's stomach pitched. For the life of her, she couldn't pick up the food and take a bite. Not with Rex still missing.

Tears pricked the backs of her eyelids and the panic that had been dogging her since Rex had run off flared again. She, Grace, Carson, Phoebe and Heidi had spent hours and hours looking for the dog all over Moonlight Cove in the pouring rain, calling his name until their voices were hoarse. Nothing. Not even a spotting.

Where could he be?

"Not hungry?" Grace asked from where she hovered nearby, clearly trying to pretend she was puttering around the kitchen rather than keeping an eye on Ally.

"I'm sorry, no," Ally replied, her voice scratchy. "Would it be okay if I wrap it up and eat it later?" Although she was doubtful she'd be able to eat at all unless they found Rex.

And if they never did? Tears welled and ran down her cheeks. She said a silent prayer for Rex's safe return.

"Of course," Grace murmured as she took the plate. "Can I get you anything else?"

Ally rose, unable to sit when Rex was out there, lost and wet and alone. "No, thank you," she said. "I think I'm going to go back out. Do you mind if I borrow your car again? I want to check the beach one more time." Rex loved the beach, and it seemed logical that he'd go there. Although a dog didn't need to act logical at all.

"Go right ahead," Grace said, pointing to the key hook on the wall. "I'll head back into town in Hugh's car to look there, and he can hold down the fort here." Hugh hadn't been cleared by his doctor for much physical activity since his procedure, so he'd been staying home to coordinate search efforts and watch Sadie and the puppies. Turned out Mr. Sellers was quite enamored of the puppies, Allison in particular, and he spent a lot of time in the whelping room, holding and cuddling the baby dogs.

"Okay," Ally said, her voice breaking.

Grace came over and enfolded her in a hug.

Ally automatically stiffened but then let herself relax and draw on the comfort Grace was offering. She hugged Grace back, and immediately some of her anxiety eased.

"Don't worry," Grace said, rubbing Ally's back. "We'll find him."

"I hope so," Ally replied huskily. "I don't know what I'm going to do if I lose him."

"You're not going to lose him."

Drew's voice jolted through Ally, and she lifted her head with a jerk, blinking.

There he stood in the door leading from the kitchen to the garage. Truly a sight for her teary eyes.

Ally pulled away from Grace, her knees quivering. "Wh…what are you doing here?" she managed to croak out.

He moved into the kitchen, and it was all she could do not to fling herself into his arms and beg him never to leave again. But she resisted, still so unsure about letting herself go to that place, so scared to let him close to her heart.

"Mom called and told me Rex was missing, so I'm here to help find him."

Ally shot a look at Grace and frowned. Grace simply shrugged as if to say, *I called him anyway.*

Focusing her attention back on Drew, Ally said, "What about the Academy?"

"There will be other academies," he said. "There's only one Rex."

"You gave up Academy to come back here and look for Rex?" Ally whispered. No one had ever given up anything for her. Rather, they'd given up on her. Left her to fend for herself. But not Drew. Wow.

"Yes, I did. I know how important he is to you, and I wouldn't have felt right not coming back."

Ally's throat clogged and she couldn't speak. Instead, she just nodded as her brain spun around and around with the significance of what Drew had done.

He'd sacrificed his spot at the Academy for her! Unbelievable. Ally just stared at him, too shocked to formulate any kind of coherent response.

In the silence that ensued, Grace took over. "Okay, so we have an extra pair of eyes and ears." She looked at Drew. "Ally was just on her way to the beach. Do you want to go with her so you can cover more ground?"

He held up his car keys. "Sounds like a plan." His eyes found Ally. "You ready?"

"Yes, yes, I am," she managed to shove out.

"Then let's go find your dog," he said. He turned and headed out into the garage.

Ally just stared at the door for a second, her jaw slack, trying to comprehend what Drew had given up to be here. He'd walked away from his dream, his future. For her.

Ally's heart expanded and warmth filled her chest.

"Now, that's devotion," Grace said, her voice echoing an obvious smile.

Yes, it was. Devotion such as Ally had never known, or imagined. What did Drew's gesture mean in the long run? And how did it change things between her and Drew? *If* it changed things at all?

She had no idea. But what she did know was that with Rex still on the loose, now wasn't the time to dissect his actions or her reactions.

Eventually, she was going to have to face reality regarding her and Drew. No matter how much she wanted to ignore the truth to keep her heart safe. The seed had been planted, and it was going to be impossible to ignore the flower once it bloomed.

She only hoped she could make the right decision in the end.

Drew pulled his truck into the deserted parking lot adjacent to the main stretch of Moonlight Cove Beach. The windshield wipers whipped back and forth, barely able to clear the rain that fell in a soggy torrent from the gunmetal-gray skies above.

He put the truck in Park, turned off the ignition and

then regarded Ally in the passenger seat, drinking in the sight of her as if he hadn't see her in a year. Even though she was clearly stressed out, and had her hair pulled back into a haphazard ponytail, she was still the most beautiful woman he'd ever seen, both inside and out.

Forcing himself to focus on the task at hand, Drew said, "We'll find Rex."

She turned a tearstained face his way, blinking rapidly. "I'm not so sure. He's been gone a whole day already," she said in a husky whisper. Her swollen, red eyes were a testament to how upset she was about her beloved Rex.

Drew's chest squeezed, and he wished he could make Rex appear and wipe the agony from her face. Her pain was his. "I wish you'd called me sooner."

"I didn't want to distract you. Today was supposed to be a big day for you." She gave him a trembling smile. "I still can't believe you came back."

"I care about you, and Rex, too," he said."

"Well, whatever the case, I appreciate your coming back," she said solemnly.

"Just try to keep me away," he said, catching her gaze and holding it.

She stared back for a moment, and he knew it wouldn't take much for him to get lost in those gorgeous green eyes. She blinked and then sucked in a quick breath. Then her jaw tightened and she yanked her gaze away, breaking their connection. Up went that wall of hers—he hated that thing, how effectively it kept him at bay.

A familiar ache throbbed beneath his breastbone. Maybe that was a permanent affliction.

She pointed out the window. "Um…we should get a move on."

Guess he couldn't blame her for wanting to proceed with the search for Rex. He corralled his thoughts and said, "Yeah." He glanced north. "We can cover more ground if we split up."

She gave him an impersonal nod that landed like a kick to his gut. "Sounds good." Then she quickly flipped the hood up on the rain jacket she'd borrowed from Mom and exited the truck.

Reminding himself that it was all about Rex right now, Drew shrugged off his bruised feelings. Hastily he shoved a Mariners cap Seth had given him onto his head before following her out into the rain. The ever-present coastal wind sliced across his face, and he yanked on his hat to be sure it sat securely on his head.

She shoved her hands into her jacket pockets. "I'll go south and you go north, okay?" Her face looked pale and drawn underneath the big hood.

"All right. Has anyone looked in the woods on the north end?" Moonlight Cove Beach bordered a wooded area thick with conifers—spruce, cedars and firs. "Might be a good place for a scared dog to hide."

She shook her head. "Not yet."

"I'll head there, then. Call me if you find anything, all right?"

Another stiff nod. "Sure. You do the same, all right?"

"Okay." He regarded her. "Don't worry, we'll find him."

She rolled her lips inward and closed her eyes, furrowing her brow. Tears leaked from underneath her

eyelids. "I hope you're right," she said, her voice just a whisper in the wind.

Again, her agony hit him like the stinging spray from a fire hose. Without thinking, he stepped forward to give her a comforting hug, and just to have her close for a brief moment. She froze as his arms went around her and stood there like a concrete statue.

Yeah. Message received. This woman didn't want him, and she never would.

With an ache spreading through him as real as the tide pulling at the ocean just a hundred yards in front of him, he stepped back and let her go. A part of him expected her to topple to the ground and shatter into a million pieces, just as an off-balance statue would.

But she didn't topple. Or shatter. She was unbreakable. She simply gave him an impassive look and, before he could get words out around the clog in his throat, she turned and headed toward the beach. Her steps picked up as she neared the sand, and she called Rex's name. Her voice was carried up and away on the wind, hopefully to Rex's ears.

Drew watched her go, a small dark figure in the rain, her shoulders hunched, as if the weight of the world rested there.

A weight she didn't want to share with him, or anyone, in any kind of meaningful way. That was the bottom line here, and the sooner he accepted that sobering truth, the sooner he could move on. Somehow.

With a snort he refocused his thoughts on his mission—to find Rex and bring him back to Ally—and started jogging north, calling Rex's name as he went.

As he hit the beach, he noted that, not surprisingly given the crummy weather, it stood empty. He scanned

up and down the waterline, over the large gray logs the tide had beached, looking for anything unusual.

Wanting to be closer to the water, and on harder sand, he jogged toward where the tide broke. A trio of gulls soared above his head on the stiff breeze, cawing, as if they were laughing at him from their vantage point high in the air.

He grimaced, not sharing their delight in the slightest way, although he'd kill for a bird's-eye view right about now.

Drew saw the forest looming in the distance, a green smudge above the rocky coastline, and picked up the pace, sticking close to the waterline for several minutes, praying he'd find some sign of Rex. Anything.

When the forest was a hundred yards or so off to his right, hugging the curving coastline, he headed inland, moving quickly even when the wet sand became harder to move through.

After walking against the wind for a few minutes, which made his breathing ragged, he reached the large rocks that separated the beach from the woods. He and Seth used to play here as kids, pretending the rocks were their pirate ships, so Drew knew his way around.

He clambered over the rocks, shouting Rex's name as he headed toward the path that led into the forest and then onto a smaller, more secluded section of Moonlight Cove Beach farther down. It was only accessible from here and a little-used forest service road.

The path was less obvious than it used to be, but still clear, although the tree limbs hung lower than he remembered. Maybe he was just taller now. Conifer needles and pinecones littered the ground, muffling

his footsteps as he hurried down the path, scanning left and right, calling Rex's name.

Just as he was about to reach the end of the path that led onto the other section of beach, a sound drifted to him on the wind. He stopped dead and cocked his head, listening. Yes! There it was again, to his right, something that sounded like a...whimper?

Homing in on the sound, he headed into the trees, his eyes searching as another whimper sounded, closer now. His heart thumping, he continued on, pushing tree limbs out of his way.

He came to a clearing and stopped, looking around... and there, lying in a heap on the ground, lay a panting, whining Rex. The poor guy had some serious-looking scratches on his left flank and was bleeding.

His breath coming fast and hard, Drew charged forward, then hit the brakes, pretty sure Rex wouldn't take too kindly to Drew touching him, especially when the dog was injured and clearly in pain. But...what else could he do? Rex needed help, and fast. That wound looked life-threatening, and who knew how long he'd been lying here, injured.

Unsure of Rex's reaction, but driven to help him, Drew slowly moved forward. "Hey, Rex, old buddy. Looks like maybe you got tangled up with a coyote."

Rex whined as his black eyes met Drew's.

Drew crept forward a bit more, his hand outstretched. "That's it, boy," he crooned. "Everything's gonna be just fine...."

Rex watched him intently as he drew near.

With infinite care, Drew made his way around to Rex's left side and crouched down when he was close

enough to touch the dog. "I'm here to help, boy. I'm here to help."

Rex whined. Did he understand? Drew, and his fingers, hoped so. One bite from those teeth could cause him serious injury.

Steeling himself to pull away quickly if need be, Drew reached out a slightly shaking hand, holding it high so Rex would see it coming.

Drew kept his eyes on Rex's face, alert for signs of fear or defensiveness. Just as his hand closed in, Rex looked up at Drew, and, amazingly, trust shone in his dark, pain-laced eyes.

Stunned—this from a dog that had been vicious in the past—Drew gently laid his hand on Rex's shoulder. "I'm here, Rex. You can relax now."

With what sounded like a combination sigh and whimper, Rex relaxed as Drew stroked his smooth fur. The dog kept his eyes on Drew, and again, complete and utter trust and faith emanated from his gaze.

Utter trust and faith. The kind that transcended fear and defensiveness and opened hearts to embrace and let in what had hurt in the past. What had wounded, seemingly irreparably.

But Rex had shown Drew that those wounds weren't beyond repair—as long as there was enough trust and faith to carry one beyond the pain and worry to the reward on the other side.

A stunning realization blasted through Drew. He hadn't had the same kind of faith in Ally. Or in himself, really. He'd used her fears, and his own, to insulate his heart. To keep it safe. Unscathed. But despite his efforts, it hadn't worked. Sitting here with Rex, Drew saw

now that he'd opened his heart after all. Everyone—Seth, Carson, Mom, Dad—had been right.

Drew loved Ally, deeply, irrevocably, passionately. And he needed to take a cue from Rex's reaction and have faith in Ally, and in his own undeniable love for her.

Drew should have fought for a future for him and Ally, not let his doubts and uncertainties hold him back from admitting the truth to himself, and to Ally. Good or bad, he saw now that acknowledging his love and telling her was the right path, no matter what the outcome.

"Well, Rex, as soon as we get you to the vet and fixed up, I'm going to tell Ally I love her." He stroked Rex's neck. "How does that sound to you?"

Rex whined. Good, he approved. With a love to last a lifetime on the line, how could Drew not heed the amazing lesson Rex had taught him?

Chapter Sixteen

With her heart in her throat, Ally rushed out into the vet's parking lot as soon as she spotted Seth's truck pull in.

Drew had called a short time ago and told her he'd found Rex in the woods north of the beach, injured from what looked like an encounter with a coyote but definitely alive. All business, Drew had quickly informed her that he was calling Seth to come get him and Rex in his truck, since Seth was familiar with the secluded forest service road that was the beach's only access route.

Together they'd decided to call Grace and ask her to pick up Ally at the beach and take her to the vet's office. Drew and Seth would then meet them there. They would pick up Drew's car at the beach later.

Ally had agreed without arguing, even though all her instincts has screamed to get to Rex as soon as possible. And after she'd hung up, she'd stood on the beach, looked up to the cloud-strewn sky and thanked the Lord for leading Drew to Rex.

Grace had arrived at the beach in record time and

hastily driven Ally to the vet, but had taken off right away to go to Mr. Sellers' follow-up appointment at the hospital. Ally had waited inside the vet's office for the longest half hour of her life.

And now, here they were, two men and her dog, safe and hopefully sound. She sobbed in relief and was headed for the back crew cab door of Seth's truck before he'd even pulled to a full stop.

Drew hopped out of the front passenger seat. "Hold on," he said, blocking the back door.

"What?"

His gaze held hers. "He's injured pretty badly."

Her eyes burned and her throat went tight. "I can handle it," she said with a lift of her chin. "He needs me."

Drew stared at her for a long moment, unblinking, then tilted his head in acquiescence and opened the crew cab door.

Rex lay there on a blanket, panting, his right back leg scratched and bloody. Tears burst forth and rolled down her cheeks. "Oh, Rexy, what happened, you naughty dog?"

He whined, his eyes on her, and she leaned in and stroked his head. "Don't worry, we'll get you all fixed up." Then a distressing thought occurred to her and her tummy plummeted to her feet. She turned and looked at Drew. "Um…I can't afford to pay the vet."

"Don't worry, I'll cover it," he said.

Her heart melted. "I'll pay you back—"

"Don't worry about it."

She nodded; it wasn't the time to argue, though she *would* pay him back eventually. How had she been

lucky enough to have this wonderful man come into her life?

Seth appeared by Drew's side. "Hey, Ally." He looked at Drew. "You ready to carry him in?"

Seth nodded. "Let's do this."

Ally moved out of the way and let the two men work the blanket out of the truck with Rex still on it so he could remain lying down. Rex whimpered but otherwise cooperated. When they had him out of the truck, Ally walked alongside them, her hand on Rex's head to comfort him.

When they got to the door, Dr. Norman held it open. "Bring him in," he said as the wind blew his short blond hair around.

Once they were all inside, he said, "Follow me to the back." He looked at Ally. "I think you ought to stay put."

"But—"

"Believe it or not it's easier on the pet when the owner isn't there," he said kindly. "I know it's hard, but I promise, we'll take good care of him and let you know how he's doing as soon as possible."

"Oh." She blinked. "Okay." It was all about Rex. She fell back and pointed to a vinyl-covered bench near the door. "I'll sit here."

Dr. Norman nodded. "Great."

Holding back a sob, she watched Seth and Drew carry Rex away.

Ally's shaking legs gave out and she sank down onto the bench, blinking back tears, which seemed to be in endless supply since Rex had run off.

A young, dark-haired woman dressed in a pink

sweater appeared behind the reception desk. "Can I get you anything?" she asked. "Tea? Coffee? Water?"

Ally shook her head. "No, thank you. I'm fine."

But she wasn't fine at all, not with the ball of dread coiling in her tummy like a snake. What was she going to do if Rex didn't make it? His injury looked brutal...

Seth and Drew came back out, their expressions grim.

Ally stood, her hands clenched at her waist.

"I have to get home," Seth said. "I told Kim I'd take Dylan to a movie so she can rest a bit."

Ally touched his arm. "Thank you so much for your help." She was touched by how kind everyone in Moonlight Cove had been to her. She'd been a stranger not so very long ago.

"No problem. Glad I was available."

"Me, too," she replied with a small smile.

"Keep me posted, okay?" Seth said to Drew.

"Will do."

With a wave, he disappeared out the door.

Ally watched him go, then turned her watery gaze to Drew.

His eyes full of softness, he stepped forward, his arms outstretched. "Come here."

Without a thought as to why she shouldn't, she stepped into his embrace with a snuffle, needing his comfort, his support, so much more than she needed distance. His fresh, clean scent and strong arms surrounded her, and she felt his heart beating steadily against her. It all calmed her, gave her hope, made her feel that she was exactly where she belonged. Right here, in the circle of his arms, able to handle anything life threw her way.

Oh, my. Yes. This was where she wanted to be. Close to him, drawing on his strength, depending on him to help her through. She'd never had that, ever, and suddenly she wanted it so badly she shook with need.

He tightened his embrace, tucking her up against him.

Her heart pulsed in time with his, knowing he was near. And there for her no matter what. Hadn't he proved that today?

"I've got you," he said next to her ear, his warm breath washing over her.

Yes, he did have her. Completely.

His hands rubbed up and down her back in a comforting sweep and she pressed closer still, never wanting to let him go. How could she when it would be like cutting off a piece of herself?

Goose bumps swept up from her toes to the top of her head, setting little fires along the way. And the truth seared its way into her consciousness like a brand.

She loved him. With her whole heart, unequivocally. She hadn't wanted to love him. But she did.

She'd fallen deeply in love with Drew Sellers.

There, she'd admitted it. Smiling against his chest, she breathed in Drew's smell, savoring the feeling of being safe in his arms, of depending on him for whatever she needed.

But what if he didn't share her feelings?

Anxiety bit hard, and she tightened her arms around his waist as if she could tie him to her with just a gesture. But, of course, she couldn't. He was free to do whatever he wanted. Stay or leave. Love her, or not. But she had to take a risk and tell him. The reward was worth the risk.

She was sure of it.

* * *

Two hours after he and Seth brought Rex to the vet, Drew sat in the waiting room, Ally's hand clenched tightly in his. She was holding it together pretty well, considering that Dr. Norman had had to do emergency surgery on Rex to repair the damage to his left side.

She'd been a trembling mess when Drew had taken her in his arms earlier. And it had felt so good for her to be there. And even better that she had let him be there for her.

Her walls seemed to be dropping. But far enough to allow him into her heart?

He chewed on his cheek. Either way, he had to come clean with her, had to have the kind of trust and faith in her that Rex had had in Drew. Confessing his feelings was a risk, sure. But after all that had happened, putting everything on the line was better than giving up.

Better than watching Ally walk away without knowing she had his heart.

He'd wasted so much time already, running scared, making excuses. That would end today. As soon as they had news of Rex, Drew would tell Ally how he felt about her. Hopefully, it would be good news all around. If not…well, he'd deal, knowing that at least he'd given himself and Ally a chance, instead of giving in to his fears. Either way, he'd be there for her.

Just then, the door to the back opened and Dr. Norman stepped out, a surgical mask hanging from his neck.

In tandem, Drew stood with Ally. Her hand tightened even more on his, until he was sure she was cutting off his circulation.

Dr. Norman met them in the middle of the room. "Well, it's good news."

Drew heard Ally let out a breath.

"I was able to repair all the damage—it *was* a coyote bite, by the way—and with some recovery time, Rex will be just fine."

Relief spread through Drew as Ally sobbed and her hand went slack in his grip. "Oh, thank You, Lord, thank You," she whispered hoarsely.

Drew put his arm around her, her relief his own.

Dr. Norman ran a hand through his hair and went on. "I'd like to keep him overnight, and then he should be able to go home tomorrow."

"Can I see him?" Ally asked, her voice laced with tempered anxiousness.

Dr. Norman nodded. "Yes, when he's out of the anesthesia and more alert in an hour or so."

Drew looked at Ally, noting her pale cheeks, sagging shoulders and the faint smudges under her eyes. "Why don't we go get some fresh air and then come back."

"O…okay." Ally's eyes drifted longingly to the door that would lead her to Rex.

"Sounds like a plan," Dr. Norman said. "We'll see you back here in an hour, give or take." He turned and disappeared behind the door.

"He's in good hands," Drew told her. "Dr. Norman is one of the best vets on the Washington Coast. I think it would do you good to clear your head."

"I guess I could leave Rex."

He opened the door and gestured her through. He followed her outside, pleased to note that the rain had stopped and some of the gray clouds looming in the dis-

tance seemed to be breaking up. Maybe the sun would shine today after all.

But he held back; he didn't want to confess his love in the vet's parking lot. Guess he had a romantic streak somewhere inside. But the beach was only a few blocks away....

"Let's walk." Taking her hand, he tugged her toward the beach, suddenly anxious to tell her how he felt. Now that he'd realized he loved her and wasn't going to give up without a fight, he didn't want to waste any more time.

She trotted to keep up. "Where are we going?"

"The beach," he told her.

"Why?"

"Well, aren't you just Miss Inquisitive today?" he said, grinning.

"Yes, I am." She stopped and shot him a suspicious look. "What's going on?"

"I just want to see the ocean, all right?" he said, tugging on her hand.

"Why?" She dug in her heels again and looked sideways at him, her green eyes narrowing. "I thought we were going to hang around here."

Exasperation prodded at him. "We were—"

"So why are we—"

"Because I don't want to tell you I love you in a vet's parking lot, that's why."

Her eyes went hugely round and her mouth fell open. She stared at him for a good long time and then squeaked, "You love me?"

He sighed. Vet's parking lot. So be it. "Yes, I do. I have for a while. But my feelings scared me, and I didn't want to admit that I loved you." With his heart

in his throat, he waited, hoping she didn't run screaming for the hills.

She regarded him seriously for a long moment. "Love is scary, isn't it?"

All he could do was nod. And hope she returned his feelings.

She stepped closer, her eyes trained on him. "Do you know how I know that?"

He shook his head, his throat so tight he didn't trust himself to speak.

"Because I've been scared to death of falling in love, too."

"And?" he pushed out.

"And..." A slow yet brilliant smile blossomed on her face. "I finally figured out after you left and I was so lost when Rex went missing that being without you scared me more than loving you. And when you came back, just for me, well...that's when my heart was toast, and I knew I could never live without you."

Hope crested like a wave in his heart. "Does that mean what I think it means?"

She moved closer, one step, two, three, and then she was there, right in front of him, her gorgeous green eyes shining like emeralds. She took both of his hands in hers. "What it means is that I love you, too, Drew Sellers, and I always will, and I'm done letting my fear control me." She bestowed upon him the most beautiful smile he'd ever seen. "Guess we were both chickens."

Joy tinged with absolute relief jetted through him. "Should we be making chicken sounds?"

One eyebrow went up. "How about you just kiss me instead?"

Sparks shot through him as he drew her into his

arms. "That's the best idea you've had all day." Then he dropped his head and kissed her, his hands coming up to cradle her head. And everything in his world was suddenly, wonderfully right.

A long time later—well, maybe only a few minutes— the sound of a car's horn honking startled both of them apart. But not enough to make him let go of her. Oh, no. From here on out, he was never letting her go.

He and Ally turned as a blue sedan pulled up. Mom and Dad.

Mom jumped out from the driver's seat seconds after the car stopped. "Does this mean what I think it means?" she asked, her mouth split into a huge grin.

Dad got out of the car, moving a bit slower, but moving.

Thank You, Lord, for taking care of my dad.

"After my appointment, Grace insisted on driving down here to check on Rex," Dad said, shaking his head. "How is he?"

"He's going to fully recover," Ally said.

"Good, good," Dad replied.

"Any other news?" Mom's gaze darted back and forth between Drew and Ally, one eyebrow arched high. "What about you two?"

Drew looked at Ally, grinning like a lovesick fool. Which he was.

Ally's eyes glowed softly, so full of love he almost quit breathing. "I love her," he said. Amazing how the uncomplicated truth was so obvious now. So…perfect.

"And?" Mom said, turning her attention to Ally.

Ally shrugged. "And I love him," she said, simple as that.

"Yippee!" Mom crowed and then hugged both him

and Ally at the same time. Then she pulled back and rubbed Ally's arm. "Welcome to the family, Ally."

Ally's eyes glittered with sudden tears, and Drew felt his own eyes burn. He knew how much she wanted the family she'd never had.

Dad came over and clapped him on the back. "Great news, son." His eyes twinkled. "Remember I told you I'd put out some feelers about fire department jobs around here?"

Drew nodded.

"Well, turns out Steve Carroll's cousin is the fire chief over in Pacific Beach. He might have a slot available in a few months."

Wow. Words failed Drew for a long moment. Pacific Beach was only a twenty-minute drive up the coast, an easy commute, meaning he and Ally could stay in Moonlight Cove.

"Actually, I think you should go back to Atherton, either now if they'll have you, or whenever the next Academy is," Ally said.

He swung his gaze to her. "You do?"

"I do." She took his hand and looked right into his eyes, her gaze steady and true. "It's your dream, and you should have it."

His heart turned over. "Are you sure? It would mean having a long-distance relationship."

"I know." She stepped close, her arms going around his waist. "But I have faith in our love, and I trust you, and I truly believe what we have is strong enough to withstand a separation."

He pressed his lips to her forehead, so glad he'd finally had a little faith. "Have I told you lately that I love you?"

"Why, yes, you have, sir." A teasing smile lit her face. "And I expect to hear it often from now on."

He kissed her. "And I'm more than happy to oblige."

Dad horned into Drew and Ally's little world. "Whatever you decide, I'm glad to hear that you two worked things out."

"Oh, me, too," Mom added, putting her arms around Dad. "Looks like we've all had a lesson or two on faith and trust, haven't we?"

Seeing his parents back together had Drew's eyes burning. "I guess we have." He blinked a few times, then looked down at the woman he loved. His heart was fuller than it had ever been. "Welcome to my life."

"And welcome to mine," she replied, her eyes shining with a love and devotion that humbled Drew.

He took her back into his arms then, breathing in the scent of her hair, feeling her heartbeat, her strength and all the other wonderful things he loved about her.

He couldn't think of another place he'd rather be.

* * * * *

Dear Reader,

Welcome to Moonlight Cove! I'm so glad you have joined me in this quaint little beachside town where love and faith blossom.

Drew Sellers was first introduced in *Family to the Rescue* (Book One, Moonlight Cove) as the hero Seth's best friend. I always intended to give Drew his own book and happily ever after—such a great guy deserves nothing less—but it took me a while to create a heroine worthy of him. I think Ally York is the perfect love interest for Drew—strong, sassy and compassionate. I hope you enjoyed their love story!

I've wanted to write a book about a dog rescuer for quite some time, and Ally seemed like a good fit. I love dogs—I have two of my own, both poodles—and really enjoy writing about the unique bond between dogs and their owners. My hat is off to dog rescue organizations; they think with their hearts to save our canine friends, and I can't imagine a better goal. As Ally believes, dogs offer unconditional love, and I share her belief wholeheartedly.

I will have more Moonlight Cove books coming out soon—I have lots of ideas for future heroes and heroines—so please, stay tuned. I love writing about this town, and look forward to creating more faith-filled love stories for your reading pleasure.

Blessings,

Lissa

Questions for Discussion

1. Drew readily offers Ally a place to stay after the fire. Since she is a stranger, is this a wise move? Why or why not? If not, what are his other options? Would it have made more sense for him to find her another, less personal, place to stay?

2. Ally has strong faith, despite what she's been through. Why do you think she keeps her faith in God instead of being more like Drew, whose faith wavers during tough times? How have you managed to keep your faith in challenging times?

3. Drew's mom, Grace, is good at shutting conversations down, and at hiding the truth of the situation with her and Drew's dad, Hugh. Discuss why you think she does this, and how she could have handled this differently, along with the pros and cons of a different reaction.

4. Ally longs for a family of her own, yet feels that dream is so far out of her reach it would never be a reality. Given her backstory, is this an understandable reaction? Would it have been more realistic to have her swing the other way and doggedly pursue building a family of her own? Or would a more middle-of-the-road reaction have been more believable? Discuss your answer, and how traumatic events in your past may have swayed your ability to be objective about future decisions.

5. Drew puts off becoming a full-time firefighter because of Hugh's expectation that Drew work in the

family business. Discuss whether you think this is a wrongheaded reaction by Drew, or whether it is justified, given his father's wants and needs. Also talk about a time when you put your own dreams aside for the benefit of someone else, and how that worked out in the end.

6. Ally's walls tremble when Drew saves the last puppy born, prompting her to open up more than she usually would. Is this a believable reaction? Why or why not?

7. Drew doesn't want to form ties in Moonlight Cove because he is planning on leaving, yet he lets Ally get under his skin anyway. How could he have kept her at arm's length more effectively? Should he have stayed away from his parents' house? Kept his and Ally's interaction less personal? Discuss.

8. Ally finds strength when she hears about Heidi's story. Discuss how someone else's reaction to a traumatic event, and strength—or lack of it—has helped you through a rough time.

9. Out of pride, Drew's dad keeps the truth about the state of the business a secret from everybody. Is this an understandable decision, or is it just wrong? Or somewhere in between? Discuss how someone in your life has kept something from you with good intentions, and how the revelation of the truth affected your relationship with that person.

10. After Drew's dad tells him the truth—that the business is on the brink of failing—Drew feels

guilty about his plans to leave town, and he is going to turn down the opportunity to go to the Fire Academy. Is this a justified reaction? Why or why not? Would it have been more realistic for him to pursue a job that would both assuage his guilt and still fulfill his dream?

11. Drew is going to tell Ally he loves her, but doesn't when he finds out that she never wants to fall in love. Is it weak of him to hold back his declaration? Or is it justified, given what is at stake? Discuss a situation in which you have held back something important, and why you did so. What was the outcome of your decision?

12. Drew's dad cuts off communication with his wife when she questions his fidelity. Is this an overreaction, or is it appropriate, given the seriousness of her doubts? How might better communication have helped avoid their rift? When is withdrawing emotionally a justified reaction? Ever?

13. Grace calls Drew when Rex goes missing, despite Ally's wish that Grace not contact Drew. Is Grace wrong for bringing him into the loop? Why or why not? Is going against someone's wishes ever justified? What kinds of situations would excuse this kind of action? Discuss.

14. After his heart problems come to light, Drew's dad has an epiphany and decides to merge his business with his biggest rival's. Discuss his decision, and whether it surprised you or not. Was he sacrificing his pride by doing this, or simply making a solid,

necessary decision in light of the situation? Also discuss your reaction to Hugh's firing of Drew.

15. When Rex lets Drew help him, Drew realizes he needs to have faith in Ally. Is this an effective way to prompt his final epiphany? If not, what would have been more effective? In addition, talk about how an unexpected event or reaction from a surprising source has helped you make a difficult decision

COMING NEXT MONTH from Love Inspired®
AVAILABLE MAY 21, 2013

PLAIN ADMIRER
Brides of Amish Country
Patricia Davids
Joann Yoder lost her dream home when the boss's nephew took her job. Only her secret pen pal understands her feelings. What'll happen when she discovers he is her Plain admirer?

SEASIDE BLESSINGS
Starfish Bay
Irene Hannon
When Kristen Andrews is unexpectedly reunited with the daughter she gave up for adoption, her tough-on-the-outside new landlord can't help being pulled into her life....

THE FIREMAN'S HOMECOMING
Gordon Falls
Allie Pleiter
Clark's and Melba's pasts are tangled by a family secret. Can they find the grace and love to win a future together?

COURTING HOPE
Jenna Mindel
Trying to move on after a family tragedy, Hope Peterson is shocked to learn that the new minister is the one man she can't forgive...and the only man she's ever loved.

RESTORING HIS HEART
Lorraine Beatty
When she agreed to help the handsome daredevil restore the town landmark he destroyed, Laura Durrant never expected to lose her heart to the man she discovers he is inside.

REUNITED WITH THE SHERIFF
Belle Calhoune
While seeking redemption for past wrongs, Cassidy Blake reconnects with her first love, Sheriff Tate Lynch. But a shocking secret from the past may doom their second chance at love.

Look for these and other Love Inspired books wherever books are sold, including most bookstores, supermarkets, discount stores and drugstores.

LICNM0513

REQUEST YOUR FREE BOOKS!

2 FREE INSPIRATIONAL NOVELS

PLUS 2
FREE
MYSTERY GIFTS

Love Inspired

SPECIAL EXCERPT FROM

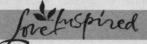

What happens when opposites attract?

Read on for a sneak peek at
SEASIDE BLESSINGS by Irene Hannon,
available June 2013 from Love Inspired.

Clint Nolan padded barefoot toward the front of the house as the doorbell gave an impatient peal. After spending the past hour fighting a stubborn tree root on the nature trail at The Point, he wanted food, not visitors.

Forcibly changing his scowl to the semblance of a smile, he unlocked the door, pulled it open—and froze.

It was her.

Miss Reckless-Driver. Kristen Andrews.

And she didn't look any too happy to see him.

His smile morphed back to a scowl.

Several seconds of silence ticked by.

Finally he spoke. "Can I help you?" The question came out cool and clipped.

She cleared her throat. "I, uh, got your address from the town's bulletin board. Genevieve at the Orchid recommended your place when I, uh, ate dinner there."

Since he'd arrived in town almost three years ago, the sisters at the Orchid had been lamenting his single state. Especially Genevieve.

But the Orchid Café matchmaker was wasting her time. The inn's concierge wasn't the woman for him. No way. Nohow.

And Kristen herself seemed to agree.

"I doubt you'd be interested. It's on the *rustic* side," he said.

A spark of indignation sprang to life in her eyes, and her chin rose in a defiant tilt.

Uh-oh. Wrong move.

"Depends on what you mean by rustic. Are you telling me it doesn't have indoor plumbing?"

He folded his arms across his chest. "It has a full bath and a compact kitchen. Very compact."

"How many bedrooms?"

"Two. Plus living room and breakfast nook."

"It's furnished, correct?"

"With the basics."

"I'd like to see it."

Okay. She was no airhead, even if she did spend her days arranging cushy excursions and making dinner reservations for rich hotel guests. But there was an undeniable spark of intelligence—and spunk—in her eyes. She might be uncomfortable around him, but she hadn't liked the implication of his rustic comment one little bit and she was going to make him pay for it. One way or another…

Will Clint and Kristen ever see eye to eye?

Don't miss SEASIDE BLESSINGS by Irene Hannon, on sale June 2013 wherever Love Inspired books are sold!

Love Inspired

Love Is Only A Letter Away

So what if Joann Yoder's Amish community deems her a spinster? She's content to stay single. In the meantime, she's working hard to finally buy her dream house. So it's problematic when she's fired from her job to make room for the owner's nephew, Roman Weaver. His blue eyes aside, she simply can't stand him! Good thing she has the secret letters she's been exchanging with a mystery man to keep her going. But who is the man writing her letters? And could she possibly fall for him in real life, too?

BRIDES OF
Amish Country

Plain Admirer
by
Patricia Davids

Available June 2013

www.LoveInspiredBooks.com

LI0513

Love Thy Neighbor?

After years of wandering, Daisy Johnson hopes to settle in Turnabout, Texas, open a restaurant, perhaps find a husband. Of course, she'd envisioned a man who actually likes her. Not someone who offers a marriage of convenience to avoid scandal.

Turnabout is just a temporary stop for newspaper reporter Everett Fulton. Thanks to one pesky connecting door and a local gossip, he's suddenly married, but his dreams of leaving haven't changed. What Daisy wants—home, family, tenderness— he can't provide. Yet big-city plans are starting to pale beside small-town warmth….

Texas Grooms

The Bride Next Door

by

WINNIE GRIGGS

Available June 2013

www.LoveInspiredBooks.com

LIH82967